Take What You Need

ALSO BY IDRA NOVEY

NOVELS

Those Who Knew

Ways to Disappear

POETRY

Clarice: The Visitor

Exit, Civilian

The Next Country

Take What You Need

IDRA NOVEY

VIKING

VIKING
An imprint of Penguin Random House LLC
penguinrandomhouse.com

LIBRARY OF CONGRESS CATALOGING-IN-PUBLICATION DATA
Names: Novey, Idra, author.
Title: Take what you need: a novel / Idra Novey.
Description: [New York]: Viking, [2023]
Identifiers: LCCN 2022017969 (print) |
LCCN 2022017970 (ebook) | ISBN 9780593652855 (hardcover) |
ISBN 9780593652862 (ebook)
Subjects: LCGFT: Novels.
Classification: LCC PS3614.O928 T35 2023 (print) |
LCC PS3614.O928 (ebook) | DDC 813/.6—dc23
LC record available at https://lccn.loc.gov/2022017969
LC ebook record available at https://lccn.loc.gov/2022017970

Printed in the United States of America
1st Printing

Designed by Alexis Farabaugh

for Gerry and Barbara

Every day you have to abandon your past or accept it, and then, if you cannot accept it, you become a sculptor.

—LOUISE BOURGEOIS

LEAH

This morning, I read that repeating the name of the deceased can quiet the mind when grieving for a complicated person. My stepmother Jean was a complicated person. I've been reading all kinds of advice since hearing of her death. I didn't know that she'd begun to weld metal towers in her living room, towers so tall she needed a ladder to complete them. Apparently, that's how she died, slipping from one of her ladder's highest rungs.

Jean never left the town where she was born, and where I was also born, and where she became the closest version of a mother I've known. It's a town in the southern Allegheny Mountains, which have been sinking for millions of years and resemble rolling hills now more than mountains. I know uttering Jean's name won't quiet my mind any more than saying the word *mountain* will stop these hills from sinking farther.

My use of the word *stepmother*, while soothing, is wishful thinking, too. Jean left my father when I was ten and hasn't technically been my stepmother for decades. I've gone through phases of calling her up, seeking her contrarian take on things. Just as often, it's felt saner to stop all contact, and the past four years we've had none.

Despite this prolonged recent silence, she left her towers to me. I received the news from a man named Elliott, who claims he'd been living with Jean for some time. He was reluctant to elaborate on the phone, beyond explaining that he was at the hardware store when Jean fell from the ladder. He drove her to the hospital, he said, as soon as he found her unconscious on the floor.

I'm driving toward Jean's house now, trying to give this man the benefit of the doubt, to imagine him grieving for her as well. Early this morning, I rented a car near my building in Long Island City.

It takes hours to cross the tilled middle of Pennsylvania and I'm not alone in this compact rental car. I have a young son in the back seat and a husband sitting next to me who isn't from this country and has never driven into the Allegheny Mountains before. I'd planned on bringing my family here at some point, once the country was less polarized, or after Jean wrote first, or after I caved and sent a few words to her. I work all day with words, revising them in multiple languages before they move on to websites, and yet these past four years I haven't been able to move even a single sentence in Jean's direction.

Beside me in the car, my husband, Gerardo, is sighing. The road before us has narrowed to two lanes, and for several miles, we've been trapped behind a blue pickup truck with several long plastic tubes rattling around in the back.

According to the GPS, it'll now be an additional twelve minutes until we reach Jean's driveway, and conjuring her name has yet to resolve the disquiet in my mind. Each time I say Jean's name to myself, I hear her louder still, the rising pleasure in her voice when she read me fairy tales, stopping to insist that she wasn't like the stepmother in "Snow White," that she had no craving for my liver or my lungs.

All I want is to nibble at your heart, Leah, she'd tell me. You don't mind if I eat your heart sometimes, right? Just one of your ventricles?

I'd play along, tell Jean to eat my whole heart if she was hungry enough. We had such fun slipping bits of ourselves into the savage parts. I've yet to read any of those Grimm tales to my son. I've stuck to newer books for him, to stories that stir up nothing from my childhood and present no risk of Jean creeping into my voice. It's felt like a neat and necessary excision, leaving out Jean and the confusing appetites of those old tales. I'm fumbling enough already, ambling motherless into motherhood.

Except now there is no Jean. She's fallen to this odd fairy tale death while living with a man I know nothing about. I hope what Elliott said on the phone about her slipping from the ladder is true, and that Jean died in the rapture of making these towers. Maybe my grief will be easier to bear over these last few hills if I keep this fairy tale going in my mind. I know even fairy tales that bend toward mercy have their brutal twists, and there's no returning to these hills without allowing Jean to gnaw at my heart again, to chew on my ventricles like strips of venison.

In the back seat, my son, Silvestre, is restless and flailing his legs. I offer him the last of the apple slices I prepared for our long trip into these sinking mountains. I assure him this old truck with its rattling plastic tubes won't remain ahead of us forever.

JEAN

I'd had it with the new mailman. He kept peering in at me through the screen door like I was up to something indecent, sculpting cocks like Louise Bourgeois. I didn't have the forging equipment to weld anything cock-shaped. I was no Louise either. I was just trying to master the nature of a box. Everything I made was flat and six-sided, and I didn't need the new mailman snickering at any of it. I also couldn't keep the front door shut, not once the metal got molten enough to start releasing its fumes and the argon gas from the TIG torch was doing its inert magic to the air.

I tried to take the high road at first. I said please and called the new mailman by the name on his uniform. I said Kenny, could you please just leave the mail on the front steps, even if it's pouring? I told him I didn't care if my bills got soggy. Kenny said sure and then went on doing exactly what I'd asked him not to, creeping up to the screen door to spy on me.

When he got here yesterday, I was sawing the heads off a new batch of spoons. I used the spoon heads for the capsules I started brazing onto my boxes, to add a few lumps of surprise to the sides.

I knew who at the flea market tended to have silver spoons. The silver ones were far softer to saw through than stainless steel. The real fun, though, was choosing what to place inside the spoon heads before I welded the capsules shut. I sealed all sorts of things inside—bits of photos, the buds of pine cones, whatever I damn well pleased.

Oh, I'd waited so long for these freeing days—too long to put up with Kenny's mocking face. When he snickered again at the screen door, I had to march out with my bow saw and let him know I'd slice off his goddamn nose if he came onto my porch again. With half of this town packing heat when they went out for groceries, a threat with a saw seemed reasonable enough.

This morning, at the creak of somebody coming up the front steps, I grabbed my bow saw again from the workbench. I was ready to let that bastard think I meant it.

Except it wasn't Kenny. It was the woman who'd moved in next door a few months ago with two grown kids. I'd yet to speak to any of them. I'd been keeping an eye on the idle son, though, as one does when a young man moves in next door who does not appear to have a job or anything to do with himself besides sit out on the front steps, swiping at his phone screen and spitting in the grass. The daughter had more spark to her, marching off each morning to school in her purple high tops, never a minute past eight fifteen. She had darker skin, and I guessed probably a different father than her older brother.

Their mother didn't step outside much. Her arrival on my porch was the first time I'd seen her up close, her dim blue eyes and limp blondish hair. She had a depleted expression that was quite a contrast to the leaping pink dogs on her T-shirt. She tapped just once on the wooden doorframe and then waited, as she could see me gripping my saw behind the workbench as clearly as I could see her, clutching the handles of two empty plastic iced tea jugs in each of her hands.

Um, good morning . . . excuse me, she called through the door. I was wondering—

Hold on a second, I told her. I'll be right there.

It was like she was peering down my throat, how intently she was ogling my shelves and machinery. I could sense her unease growing as she took in all my Manglements, what I'd come to call my box shapes in my mind. To keep the floor clear, I'd crammed most of the smaller ones onto the wooden shelves where my mother had displayed the painted plates she'd gotten from her mother. I still had their plates—I'd just relocated them to a corner down in the cellar.

Something you need? I called to my neighbor as I stepped around the workbench. I took my time, not wanting to trip on the scraps of cowhide I kept over the floorboards to avoid any more errant sparks from my welder starting a fire. Last summer, some sparks burned a hole clear through the floor to the cellar, igniting the cushion of an old chair.

On the other side of the screen door, clutching her empty tea jugs, the woman kept gaping at my front room, nodding like she'd forgotten what she'd come up the steps to ask me. Yes, she said, yes, I was . . . ah . . . wondering if we could use your spigot. The city shut off our water.

Those bastards, I said. I'm sorry.

I placed my hand on the knob, waiting for her to back up so I could push the door open and speak to her without the grimy screen between us. She didn't step back, though, which was fine with me. I left the screen door closed—why her water bill had gone unpaid wasn't any of my business, same as my life wasn't any business of hers.

You're more than welcome to use the spigot anytime, I told her from my side of the door.

It would just be these four gallons, she said from her side, raising both hands, causing her empty plastic iced tea jugs to smack against each other.

Take whatever you need, I told her, and you don't have to come and ask. Just go ahead and fill 'em. It's fine.

The woman nodded at this, already beginning her careful retreat toward the porch steps. She didn't offer her name and I didn't ask for it—or offer her my name either. It seemed best to just let the conversation end there. I didn't want her to think she had to give me a taste of her family's problems in order to use my water.

Of course, I was being cautious for my own sake, too. Among the handful of us owners still left on Paton Street, I considered myself among the least paranoid, though I wasn't naive. She was a woman with a grown son ticking away on the front steps. We had too many young men ticking like that all over town, more than at any point in my life—their stillness felt almost cultlike, all of them hunched over, praying to nothing, and the rest of us driving by, eyeing them with sadness and dread.

With just about everyone now in the East End, it had become a nonstop eyeing-and-spying situation. No matter how often a gun went off, I couldn't get used to it. The few other owners hanging on to their homes didn't want to talk any more than I did about why we were the ones who hadn't traded up and cleared out when it was still possible, before our houses became worthless. The Section 8 families and renters were wary of us, too, not knowing which of us might be bitter and cause problems. They spied just as much on one another, arriving with their worn-out mattresses and their belongings in garbage bags. Hardly any of them lasted a year.

After the woman left, I got agitated, sorry for her and her kids, but leery, too, of what she might come over and ask for next. To clear my mind, I sat down for a moment at my laptop before getting back to the rest of the spoon heads.

In my Hotmail, I found a message waiting from Leah. Not a personal message—I only heard from her when she sent around one of her impassioned donation requests. I clicked yes every time, sometimes sending ten bucks, sometimes more. Except for a rare phone call when she was worked up about her father, I'd become a nonentity to her, former stepmother being a nonposition, with no reliable shape whatsoever. This time, Leah was after donations for kids arriving alone at the border, kids hungry and terrified enough to do such a thing. I typed in twenty, the tendons in my hands cramping as I sent my usual two-sentence reply to let her know I'd donated and that I hoped she and her husband were doing well. She rarely wrote back with more than a few lines. I'd only learned she had a husband when she sent a mass email with a picture from their honeymoon, the two of them standing together at the equator. I'd gotten the news from her group email like I was no more to her now than an acquaintance, as if all the years she'd sat on my lap had never happened, as if all the mornings she'd slipped into my side of the bed meant nothing now.

After clicking send, I had to spritz my face at the kitchen sink. Through the open window behind the faucet, I heard the glug and spurt of the spigot starting up outside. I assumed it was the mother crouching on the other side of the wall. The branches of my hydrangeas had grown out of control and I hoped they weren't poking that poor woman in the ass.

Fuckin' bushes, I heard a man swear, his voice so close through the open window it startled me.

When he erupted again, mouthing off about the spray from the spigot, I clinked two glasses in the sink. To make certain he got the message that he couldn't come over, grumbling like that every day at my spigot, I clanged a knife against one of the glasses.

The grumbling on the other side of my window stopped immediately. Only one of us had water. And it was me.

LEAH

I've missed a turn somewhere in this density of woods. The arrow on my phone indicated a road that doesn't seem to exist. Or maybe the turn was there and I just failed to spot it, caught up in the balm of improvising a possible fairy tale for Jean.

I thought I was paying close attention, searching for the turn among the stark distant homes on this road, tucked at the end of their long, tarred driveways. The open distances here feel unfamiliar to my citified mind. I have a feeling I may have turned my family around inadvertently, sent us traveling back toward the turnpike we left half an hour ago, instead of heading farther west as we intended, toward the last towns and valleys before these mountains become West Virginia.

Behind me, Silvestre is frantic for a stop. To distract him until we find the hidden turn, I put on his favorite song about unicorns, which we've played a dozen times for him already. Lulled by his unicorns, Silvestre falls quiet. In the front seat, to will a sense of calm for myself, I try to remain with the thought of Jean building towers in the living room of that grim house. What a relief it would bring for Elliott's version of events to be true, for Jean to have found a magical piece of flint in these last years of her life. Maybe she had to keep her fire contained, not knowing how others in the area would react if they saw smoke coming from a cave in the mountainside where nobody expected any sparks.

Although I know what Jean would say about my imagining her holed up on the side of a mountain. She'd despise the idea of my imagining her in the cultural equivalent of a cave. She'd say my desire to mourn her in fairy tale was a load of duck shit. She'd say, C'mon on, Leah, if you're going to grieve for me with some duck shit, why not admit to the real stuff, what we crunched over barefoot? She'd ask if I'd forgotten that creek spot she found, and I haven't. I may have chosen the clean break of silence with her these past four years, but I haven't forgotten that secluded creek, stepping through the dried-up duck shit that pebbled the entire shore. My father came along just once and called the spot too filthy to bother, said he couldn't understand what Jean found so special about it.

I understood it, though. Nobody else ever arrived besides the two of us and the ducks, the dragonflies that shimmered over the water. Jean insisted I had to get over my squeamishness, said she loved me too much to allow me to become a buttoned-up woman who couldn't get through a little dung to float in the most stunning creek around.

Over my dead body are you going to become that kind of snob, she'd tell me. You're my child now, too, not just your father's. You listening to me?

What's that? I'd answer to provoke her, running ahead into the water to splash her first.

You heard me, you little pain in the ass, she'd yell and splash me back.

She'd never state her claim on me more than once. I felt loved and lucky when she said it, that I belonged to her, standing together on that hidden shore. It still feels like a secret, stuffed down somewhere in myself, Jean's claim on me, following her down that shore my father found disgusting, enjoying the cereal-like crunch of the duck shit under my bare feet.

I felt luckier still when we'd stop at Long John Silver's on the way home for hush puppies and fried fish planks delivered through the takeout window in cardboard boats. Jean liked to tip all the crispy crumbles at the bottom of the boats into her mouth at once. I found the crumbles more delicious this way, too, and while we wiped the grease from our lips and laughed, she'd remind me that a little fib was no big deal and I'd nod in agreement, knowing she meant my father, who was going to ask if we'd gone to that filthy creek again, when he'd paid for the pool at the golf club.

The next winter, on a school day, Jean moved out of our house with no warning. I cried for her into a pillow at night so my father wouldn't hear. If he heard, he'd come into the room to assure me that a time would come when I would be relieved that Jean was no longer my stepmother. That time will come sooner than you think, he'd say, trust me. He said this often enough that such a time began to feel inevitable, when I would desire no connection to Jean at all. I got so used to avoiding any mention of her in front of my father that it's come to feel natural not to bring her up with Gerardo, or with anyone else. I hadn't expected the news of her actual death to leave me crying again at night into a pillow.

On my phone, the GPS keeps adding more miles between the direction in which we're moving and the house where Jean fell from a ladder while assembling some kind of tower taller than herself. Elliott wouldn't describe them on the phone. He just kept reiterating that there were many and they were mine.

JEAN

M y new neighbor didn't come to the door again after that one awkward conversation. Once a day, I heard him at the spigot outside my kitchen window. He usually came over around ten in the morning. I'd hear him out there, filling the four plastic iced tea containers his mother had brought with her to the door and never a jug more, unless maybe he was drawing extra water at night when I was asleep upstairs. I counted the pauses, when the water started drumming into the next container, waiting for him to fill an extra jug or two. I certainly would have, why not? I'd told his mother they could take what they needed.

Maybe she'd urged her son not to push things. Her alarm about my Manglements had been plain on her face, peering in at me behind my dad's workbench, wondering why I wasn't out crouching in a flower bed, where women my age were supposed to work out their fading beauty.

I waited for her grown son to take more. I wanted him to show a little nerve, to test me, and yet every day after the water drummed for the fourth time into his plastic gallon jugs, I'd hear the snap of the hydrangea branches as he backed away.

How three people got by on so little water I couldn't guess. I assumed they had to drink and cook with it, probably flush with it, too. From seeing the notices on other houses, I knew it wouldn't be long before someone from the city started posting hygiene risk warnings on their front door, the eviction orders coming soon after that.

I gave the idle son a nod if he was out on the steps when I pulled into the driveway. Otherwise, I kept my distance until early June, when I was arriving from my cousin Marty's scrapyard over in Deerfield. Marty ran things from Baltimore now. He'd renamed the business Levy Recycling, though it was pretty much the same junk heap it had been when I was a child and it was called Levy Metal Co. Marty's dad ran it then and gave work to my father until he mouthed off and picked too many fights. My dad was convinced my mother's family looked down on him, which they surely did, as Dave had looked down on me, and I couldn't help mouthing off and picking fights with him either.

My mother was never in the running to take on her family's scrap business. The yard had passed from son to son for a century, and now for the day-to-day operations, nobody from my mother's family got involved. Marty had found a tall, quiet man from Belarus to run things. Sergei never asked what I did with the sheet metal he loaded onto my truck. We kept our talk to size and thickness, and Sergei made sure the sheets of scrap metal he saved for me weren't heavier than what I could unload on my own, and with no trace of zinc coating that might leave me dead from fume fever.

I would have loved to get some longer pieces of scrap and scale up, weld a box big as a casket, but I'd already thrown my back out trying, which felt like blunt proof that I was just a putterer, stuck at the scale of what I could drag up the front steps.

This time, Sergei gave me some better sheet metal than usual. He'd put aside three pieces with almost no major dents and only a few patches of rust. Two of them were heavier than usual—almost a quarter-inch thick, and I was dreading the battle it would take to haul them into the house.

On the drive back from Deerfield, I tried to mentally prepare for the struggle up the front steps, to think of it as what Louise called the necessary battle with one's material. No real art, Bourgeois said, was possible without a fight with one's material. And wouldn't she know, having conquered just about everything? Steel. Marble. Pantyhose. Nightmares. Surely I could conquer a few pieces of sheet metal without tearing my shoulder from its socket.

You have to become more than yourself is what Louise said when she passed sixty-five, the station on the life train coming up for me as well, and when Louise started sculpting cocks big as boxing bags, suspending them at whatever height she wanted. Every night I sipped a few lines from her writings in bed. I had no nerve in the morning if I skipped my nightly Louise. I'd come down the stairs and somehow piss the hours away, sanding lids and sweeping the floor like my own maid.

When I pulled into the driveway with my scrap load, I saw the idle son next door was slumped on the front steps again in his unlaced construction boots, his buzzed head hanging over his spread knees. I gave him a nod as I'd been doing since he'd started drawing his family's water from my spigot. He returned the nod and lowered his head to his phone. Once I unlatched the bed of the pickup, I felt the radius of his gaze on me again while I strained to lift the top piece of sheet metal.

I assumed he was home alone. His younger sister wouldn't have returned from school yet and it seemed their mother had agreed to some kind of work at Porter's Deli up the street. In the late afternoon, I kept seeing her shuffling up their driveway with day-old hoagies, or some kind of cast-off food wrapped in the wax paper the Porters had been using for their sandwiches since I was a kid and Betsy Porter would bike past muttering something hateful at my friend Alvina and her brothers, the only Black kids on the street. I'd been the only Jewish kid. Whenever Betsy felt like it, she'd yell over for me to show her my horns.

Betsy ran the deli now, and I still would rather pour WD-40 in my coffee than walk in there for a carton of milk. I'd seen other women like this mother next door, who arrived with no car or job and agreed to whatever terms Betsy offered them. I'd see them emerge from the deli around the same time in the afternoon holding rolls of toilet paper or crushed bags of Wonder Bread. Then after a month or two they'd stop coming. I had a hunch Betsy paid them with a degrading mix of cash and unsaleable goods.

I'd rarely seen the son leave the porch. He just sat like a goose on the front steps, pecking at a bag of chips as he was now, watching me throw my back out. He just kept on watching, offering none of that brute strength that comes unbidden to young men.

Do you think maybe you could get up, I said, and give me a hand?

He rose immediately and shuffled over the uneven grass between our homes. He had the curved posture of someone accustomed to bracing for humiliation and I realized it was entirely possible he hadn't offered to help because he didn't think his offer would be welcome.

It's just three pieces of sheet metal, I told him. But be careful, they're heavier than they look, I warned as he reached the driveway.

There was nothing particularly striking about him. He was of average height and scrawny with a pale, square face and a thin scar that ran from the right edge of his chin clear up through his lower lip. His large brown eyes sat a little too close to his nose. I expected him to deal with the sheet metal in a reluctant, inefficient sort of way. But he heaved all three pieces with a swiftness that surprised me. I also got a whiff of his BO and hoped my reaction wasn't evident on my face.

You want 'em by the door? he asked.

Or just inside it, I said, if you don't mind.

And how could he mind?

I doubt I would have been so brazen if I hadn't been watching him for months, how often he sat outside quietly talking with his little sister. He could have joined the agitated crowd that gathered outside the tobacco shop down on Henley, or the dull-eyed group that loitered outside the Greyhound station, their eyes glassy from fentanyl, or junk heroin, whatever was going cheapest now.

I had yet to see him sip a beer or smoke a joint on the porch. He seemed to have a calm demeanor. I hadn't heard him yell much at his sister or mother. If I had, I wouldn't have asked for his help.

Although maybe that isn't true. My father yelled all the time and I still moved back into this house to argue with him until he died. And I'd certainly done a good bit of yelling at Leah. When she ran down the slippery tiles at the YMCA before her swim class, I shouted at her. We all shouted at our kids, threatening to take them home if they didn't listen.

At the time, I didn't recognize how much I enjoyed my place in that collective of clucking mothers on Wednesday afternoons, hearing our empty threats echo in the damp chamber of that shabby basement pool. What pleasure there had been in all that fussing over our kids, commiserating over the primal fear of being the one whose six-year-old fell and cracked her head open.

The quiet son from next door didn't say anything at first as he stepped into my house. He set down the sheet metal just inside the door, leaning the pieces against the wall. I watched him silently take in all the Manglements on the shelves, and the ones too big for the shelves I'd left sitting on the floor.

What is all this? he asked, pointing with his chin toward the shelves and then the workbench.

What do you mean? I said. Doesn't your family weld in the living room?

He pressed his lips together just slightly, not a smile but not a grimace either.

What's your name? I asked him.

Elliott, he said.

Well, I appreciate the help, Elliott, thank you, I said, hoping he would get the hint and leave. He didn't seem in the same hurry to retreat as his mother had, and he wasn't looking around with the gobbling, awful scorn of the mailman either. This Elliott had another energy to him, an openness in his gaze I hadn't expected.

I watched him take in my cockeyed box lids and the funny lumps of my capsules, bumping out like measles all over the sides.

It caused a fizz in my mind, watching Elliott step closer to my largest Manglement so far—a narrow, totem-like tower I'd left on the floor next to the window that looked out onto his house. I'd welded some of my spoon-backed capsules in a spiral, rising around the four metal sides toward the lid. I thought it was pretty cool, the sense of diagonal movement the capsules made.

I watched Elliott squint at one of the capsules on the Manglement closest to him, the sawed-off torso of a plastic soldier figurine I'd trapped inside it. I waited for him to ask about the capsule, but he didn't. He just rocked back on his boots and looked around some more, considering my tools hanging on the wall and the used welder I'd bought for my TIG gun. It occurred to me as I watched him stare at the welder how easily he could break in here, rob all this precious machinery I'd driven hours in every direction to acquire, waking at four a.m. to be among the first to arrive at the better flea markets outside Pittsburgh before the good tools and spoon sets got picked over.

That welder looks good, I told him, but it isn't worth shit. I bought it used from the widow of a guy over in Ligonier. And I got that Grizzly band saw for dirt cheap from her, too. It's ten years old but it works just fine for my purposes.

But what are they, Elliott asked softly, all them boxes?

It's just what I do, I told him instead of admitting anything I would've liked to say aloud about art requiring a degree of bullheadedness—about Agnes saying a real artist has to be able to fail and fail and still go on.

I got laid off, is what I told Elliott.

I explained I'd worked in billing at the county hospital until it shut down and we all got chucked at once and sent home.

Shit, Elliott said, running a hand over the bristle of dark hair on his buzzed head. He didn't turn toward the door to leave, though, and I couldn't help liking him for that, for staying far longer than his mother had. He'd probably arrived, though, with the advantage of her warning. Surely his mother had reported on the amount of weird crap she'd seen in here through the screen door.

This is all I got, I told him, not meaning for it to come out as a plea, but I was getting nervous at how keenly he was looking at my tools. His body odor was even more potent indoors, pungent enough to smell from the other side of the workbench. I couldn't stop eyeing the unused muscles in his shoulders. His face gave away nothing, his expression about as revealing as a shut garage door.

I was the only one among the remaining owners who hadn't put in a security system. I couldn't stand to live in a force field of paranoia, surrounded by cameras.

That yours, too? Elliott asked, pointing at the only painting in the room, a clumsy portrait I'd done of Leah from her school photo in kindergarten, with the long French braids she asked for me to put her hair in then. On warm mornings, I'd done her braids on the front porch.

Yep, all mine, I told him.

That your daughter?

I held in my breath. It was an awful, incompetent portrait, with uneven, amateurish eyes and clumped paint on one of her nostrils. Leah's thick dark bangs took up half her head. I had no gift for painting or representational art and yet once I hung up that picture of her, there was no taking her face down. In the weeks after I left her father, I'd called constantly, hoping he'd let me continue picking Leah up from school, take her for bike rides, ice cream, anything. He'd refused.

It seemed like she'd turned out just fine, though, without me. She'd gotten herself all the way to the equator. In that honeymoon photo she'd sent, I'd been surprised to see her face had become as angular as her father's, though more good-looking and feminine, with big silver earrings and her bra straps showing under her tank top. I'd stared at that photo of Leah so often and intently that I got worked up just thinking about opening it. One night, I deleted it—a stupid impulse, though it did relieve the sting of that adult face of hers that I didn't know at all.

She's all raised now, I answered in the most perky tone I could muster. She hasn't lived in Sevlick for a long time, I told him.

Lucky her, Elliott said, lowering his head, and I felt for him.

Can you cut them metal sheets with this? he asked, pointing at the sanding disk on the floor that I'd bought for the grinder. He looked up for my answer and his straight-on gaze unnerved me. I hadn't been in this house with any man but my father in such an awfully long time. My skin felt different, prickly.

That's more for buffing, I explained. But see the disk there on the grinder? That can cut a corner off easy enough.

And pretty quick, too, I'd guess, he said in the same hesitant voice, like he was unsure how to admit it any plainer, his curiosity, and a softness overtook me, one of those moments when the heart refuses to close.

Oh, you bet it cuts real quick, I told him, and it's fun as hell. Here, I'll show you.

He drew closer to the opposite side of the workbench, making it harder to ignore the smell of his body. My fingers got stiff and clumsy, clamping the small rectangle of sheet metal to the workbench. Tightening the clamp took more time than usual—I was so used to working alone.

Before clicking on the grinder, I looked up to see if I could detect any scorn on Elliott's face as he watched me. I pulled on the grinder cord, though it didn't have much give, tangled as it was, so taut the cord was floating a few inches off the ground from the workbench to the socket.

The new grinders have a safety switch that shuts it off the second you let your finger go, but I preferred this older, solid grinder, without any of the cheap plastic parts of the new ones. I'd bought myself a new one last year, not top of the line, but it had cost more than I spent on a month of groceries. The disk release button kept getting stuck and I gave up on it, switching to an older grinder I'd found at a garage sale over in Deerfield, on one of my supply trips to the scrapyard.

In two strokes, I rounded the corner of that little rectangle down to a rather smooth, even masterful curve. When I looked up, Elliott had drawn in his square jaw with what looked like genuine surprise.

Where'd you learn to do that? he asked.

YouTube.

You serious? he asked, looking back at me more openly now.

Oh, you can learn anything if you look up Weldporn on You-

Tube, I told him. How to tack-weld, how to wipe your ass. Whatever you type in, there's some eager beaver out there with a step-by-step on how to get it done. I learned as a kid, too, from my dad. He didn't mean to teach me. He only let me near his workbench if he really needed an extra pair of hands. You ever operate a grinder?

Elliott shook his head with a wistful half smile and I told him I'd give him a turn if he wanted, once he saw how I rounded the second edge. While I adjusted the clamp, I rambled about the sparks from the grinder, how their intensity changed depending on what alloys were in the scrap metal, and I liked how he didn't interrupt with some kind of put-down. Everything about his posture and attire aligned with the sort of young man who would scorn a woman my age operating a grinder and in her living room. And yet there was no meanness in his gaze, not the ruthless kind I'd learned to brace for my whole life.

As I smoothed down the second corner, it got easier to relax and stop waiting for an insult from Elliott, to tune my attention to all the evidence of my competence around us, the rows of Manglements I'd already welded, all my intricate capsules with their tiny chambers. It took skill to weld the thin metal frames that held those capsules together. For the front of them, to be able to see into the chamber, I used curved lenses extracted from old cameras I found cheap on eBay if nothing turned up at the fleas.

The inside of each capsule couldn't fit anything larger than a plastic figurine. The spoon head served as the solid back, with the camera lens for the clear front, magnifying whatever I sealed inside, which was where the fun house of the capsules happened.

Combining a sliver of a silver gelatin photo of some man's crotch with a tiny Wade porcelain pig, seeing them get weirder, magnified inside the same little chamber, that was my idea of a good time. I sealed all sorts of junk together. A milky marble with a photo of somebody's funny-looking child picking her nose.

I liked anything with an air of Cindy Sherman. Or Diane Arbus. I never ended the subscription to *Artforum* I got after college. I had a roommate at Saint Francis who turned me onto the art magazine shelf at the library. Her mother had hustled her, too, into studying business administration and being practical about her prospects. After Carol got pregnant and dropped out, I flipped through the art magazines on my own, decided I'd head to Cleveland after college, or maybe even Chicago.

I never would've moved home after graduation if my mother's MS hadn't gotten so bad. Once I'd helped her through her last stretch of life, I assumed I'd be on my way, taking my *Artforum* subscription with me—except Dave came into the hospital library, with his sharp mind and wry take on the ineptitudes of everyone. I liked his devotion to his tiny daughter. I thought he'd get less angry about losing his wife, and once he did, he'd stop belittling me so much. Or he'd just tire of making the same snide comment on how long I'd kept my *Artforum* subscription going. Nine years into marriage, though, he still couldn't let a single issue arrive without asking a question just to catch me pronouncing a name wrong and correct me. I started to hide my new issues like nudie mags, pulling them out only when I was in the bathroom or Dave was out of the house.

It caught me off guard, how fast all that history surged up

with Elliott standing next to the workbench. I resisted the urge to pause, not wanting him to think he could rattle me. I just swallowed the bile of my marriage back down and got to grinding the third corner. To reach it, I had to pull the cord a little tighter. In its knotted, jumbled state, there was hardly any slack left in the cord length. I had to yank on it to finish the corner.

Even with the cord taut as a tightrope, I rounded the edge down in three quick strokes. How's that for a graduate from You-Tube? I yelled over the grinder's roar.

Elliott laughed as he took a step forward, and it happened so fast—the grinder jerking out of my grip. I didn't even realize when it flew out of my hand that the cause might be Elliott stepping forward, bumping into the taut cord suspended half a foot off the floor in front of him.

At the blast of pain in my thigh, I clung to the edge of the workbench, blood spilling quick as paint across my pant leg. And there was the grinder blade still on and spinning across the floor like a sentient thing, its sharp whirring disk moving toward my boot.

Elliott bent to grab it and I had to shout at him he was going to lose his fingers, that he had to run and unplug it from the wall instead.

The silence after he yanked out the cord came total as an explosion. In the scream of the grinder, I hadn't been able to hear how loud the pain had become. No matter how hard I pressed on my thigh, the blood kept pulsing up, seeping between my fingers. In my head, a feeling like all the circuits shutting down.

Get a rag, I grunted to Elliott. I told him the drawer left of the sink, to grab a long one for a tourniquet. Once I felt his hands under my elbows helping me to lower myself to the ground, I realized how hard I was shaking, the pain raging clear up into my groin.

I got some gumbands to keep it tight, he said and I nodded, holding back the cry pushing at my throat. The stain darkening down my pant leg just kept expanding. Wider. Wetter. A shocking amount of blood.

Elliott looped the rag around my thigh and asked if it was tight enough.

I nodded again, though I had no idea. The blood soaked through immediately and kept coming, even after Elliott twisted the gumbands tighter and said he'd better call 911.

No, don't call those idiots! I shouted, twisting against the pain, my jaw trembling so much it was hard to get the words out. I told him I knew the crooks running the county ambulance service now. All of us in the billing department had seen the wild invoices that started coming through at the end, the invented updates to equipment that had never been bought. The drive over the mountain to Hamillville, to what was now our only hospital in the tri-county area, wasn't that far, only twenty minutes at most. I explained where to find my keys on the kitchen table.

I won't die on you, I promise, I told him.

I grabbed onto his arm as firmly as my shaky hold would allow. The press of his palm against my ribs was a welcome distraction from the pain. Even the stink of his armpits felt oddly consoling and I let my head fall against his bony chest.

So fuckin' stupid I walked into the cord, Jesus Christ, he said as he carried me out the door, and I assured him the stupidity was all mine, leaving a power cord that tangled, yanking it clear off the floor, and not warning him to look out for it.

By the front steps, my hands were too limp and slick with blood to keep any hold on the back of his neck. Deadweight was what I'd turned into by the driveway, deadweight and the mortification of it, having to be carried out of my house, a useless old creature who couldn't be trusted with her own tools.

You better tell me your name, Elliott said in a hoarse, nervous voice, releasing me onto the passenger seat with a gentleness that didn't escape me.

I'll make it, don't worry. But it's Jean. Kovacevic.

Kova what? How do you spell that? he asked and I spelled it out for him.

And you're Elliott what?

Hounslow, he said.

Well, Elliott Hounslow, sorry I got so much blood on your neck.

He joined my strained laugh and I watched him, the blood streaks down the front of his Steelers shirt as he made his way around the front of the truck to get in on the driver's side. At his hesitation to start the engine, I realized I had just assumed he would know how to drive. Even if their family didn't own a car, every kid in Sevlick got behind a wheel and learned somehow.

Elliott jerked the brakes something terrible backing out of the driveway, causing a new voltage of pain to jolt up through my leg. I groaned and he apologized.

I, ahh . . . I haven't driven in a while, he said. You want me to ask your neighbor there to take ya?

He motioned through the driver's-side window to Steve Pav-likowski, who was outside in his gray sweatpants, pouring the dregs of his coffee onto his dead lawn. I'd hated Steve since high school, hated the enormous twelve-foot sign he'd bought for his garage door: DUE TO THE HIGH PRICE OF AMMUNI-TION, TRESPASSERS SHOULD NOT EXPECT WARN-ING SHOTS.

I lied and told Elliott he was driving just fine, and he should keep on going. I forced out the words, my voice brittle as some banged-up piece of sheet metal. I watched you with those gum-bands, I told him. You're sharp, Elliott, I've got faith in you.

He didn't say anything in response. He just kept on rolling toward the corner. Maybe he was reassured, or just too scared about my dying next to him to argue. I'd stopped trying to apply pressure to the tourniquet. Whether my weak efforts had helped any, I couldn't tell. The rag, my pants, the palms of my hands, there was new blood everywhere before we'd even left the house. I felt cold, shivers like it was the middle of winter, my teeth rat-tling so much I had to hold my mouth open.

Elliott jerked the brakes even harder at the stop sign and I felt another gush, the blood warm under my fingers. I asked if I was making him nervous.

What's 'at? he asked. Nervous? I'm not fuckin' nervous. I saw my uncle misfire and shoot one of his toes off. I think you better call your daughter, though, you want me to call her?

I could've set the record straight then. But if I'd sliced into an artery and was going to hemorrhage to death before Hamillville, what did it matter? It seemed like a minor last indulgence to go on being the mother of Leah, just for this last drive with Elliott up past the Dickston Rock Quarry and over the ridge.

I'll let her know once we get there, I said. And how 'bout your mom? She's gonna wonder where you're at.

She's workin' till four, Elliott said.

Okay, then, I told him and closed my eyes. Head right when you hit Hannaford, you're doing just fine, I lied as he went on pumping the gas pedal. Making the right turn, he jerked the brakes yet again, causing such a flare of agony in my thigh I had to thrash my head to release it.

On his jerky turn at the intersection, my leg swung and crashed against the door. I swore and Elliott mumbled that this was a terrible idea. You need to go in an ambulance, he said.

You're doing fine, I lied again. Just let up on the brakes a little.

I tried to clutch my leg again, just in case it helped, trying not to pass out as Elliott went on pumping the gas pedal past the beer depot and the car dump. At Summerhill, I motioned with my limp fingers to veer left and Elliott said he knew it was left. He didn't flick on the turn signal, which didn't matter. Summerhill was empty in both directions, the only sign of life far down at the end of the street, outside the double doors of the Salvation Army—if you could call it life, that sad line for free macaroni and frozen peas. I should have left this dreary town years ago. Decades ago.

At the corner, Elliott pumped the brakes once more, and I didn't try to stop the new rush of blood, warm under my palm. To keep from passing out, I tried to call up my Agnes Martin mantra about letting expectations go—to accept inaccuracy or accept failure. Which was it? Error? Total failure?

After driving past all those motionless people outside the Salvation Army, the surrender on their faces, my mind wouldn't yield the right word from Agnes. It wouldn't deliver anything from Louise, as if their words were never meant for me in the first place, as if nothing belonged to me but this town I'd stuck to like a tick on a dog.

Dave had pushed for us to move out of Sevlick. He'd wanted better schools for Leah, had claimed keeping an eye on my dad was just an excuse, that I didn't have it in me to leave. I'd given him hell for saying that, and yet here I still was.

Elliott jerked the wheel again at the top of Summerhill, and I swore, twisting in the seat, the pain too intense to keep still.

I'm going to call an ambulance, he said, reaching for his cell phone until I flicked his hand away.

Just go easier on the turns, I'll be fine, I told him.

Talking felt good. If I kept my mouth moving, maybe I wouldn't pass out.

You know why I can't die yet? I said. Because I haven't gotten a damn thing exactly right. You ever heard of Agnes Martin? Carmen Herrera? You know how old they were before anyone gave a shit?

Up here, right? Elliott pointed to where Summerhill forked and the road tipped starkly upward over our little edge of the Allegheny Mountains that led to Hamillville and I nodded, clutching my leg as he took the turn onto Finley too hard.

You've got the hang of it now, I lied as he drove too close to the edge of the road on the next turn. There was barely any berm once the road steepened along the mountainside, the thick trunks of the oak trees flickering no more than two feet away from Elliott's window. At a downed branch, he jerked the wheel and I grabbed hold of my leg too late to steady it. Pain shuddered up into my groin and I grunted, determined to keep talking.

Sculpture is an exorcism, I muttered. It's a goddamn exorcism, and you know what? You can't stop halfway through an exorcism. You hear what I'm saying, Hounslow, you listening? That is straight from the mouth of Louise Bourgeois and she knows what she's talking about, all right? *All right?* I yelled, rolling my head toward Elliott, and he side-eyed me with alarm.

All right, all right, he repeated, and I inhaled hard, closed my eyes as the truck rocked again with the next curve around the mountainside. At least Louise was still in my head. I still had her words in there, whether she was meant to belong to me or not. Everything in me said *remain*. My mind said *remain*. My trembling thigh said it. I couldn't be done yet, not before I figured out something beyond my Manglements. Not after all those years alphabetizing files, sending out bills to patients who'd just throw them away. Dave had wanted me to quit at the hospital. Somehow I'd sensed I'd better keep that stake in the ground. Once Leah started preschool, I started filling in for whoever had a baby or took a vacation. Having the income didn't change Dave's daily nips of condescension. I hadn't seen that smallness in him at first, when he'd been curious about Bull Creek. We'd hit the fleas together for a while, taking Leah in the carrier, until Dave got tired of going, said it depressed him, watching so many broken people sell old junk to each other. Every way I'd come to seek beauty, he found a way to deflate it. We reached a real hatred by the end.

Still, I'd never thought he would be cruel enough to use Leah for revenge and forbid her to call or see me even once, knowing his daughter and I could finish each other's sentences. We'd fused as completely as if she'd shared half my particles.

God, I miss my girl! I exclaimed aloud, and Elliott asked again if I wanted to call her.

I think you should, he said, and I shook my head, told him the reception was no good up here on the ridge.

I was more careful to keep my mouth shut after that, driving on over the mountain. I kept my focus on the steady repetition of the trees, how firmly they insisted on themselves. I didn't realize I was falling forward in the seat until Elliott reached over to help.

You gonna pass out? he asked, and I said no, though the edges of my tongue felt numb and gummy. I forced my head back against the seat rest and asked him to tell me something. About his family, about anything at all.

I think I better focus on the fuckin' road, he mumbled and I didn't ask again. We were just about at the top of the ridge now, the forest denser, and I stared out with him through the windshield at the vast rolling green of the treetops, at the two hawks circling to the right of us, where the mountain fell away.

The chance of reaching the hospital alive seemed more likely with every second, with every turn Elliott made without crashing into a tree trunk or hitting anyone driving into the same sharp bend from the other direction. I hadn't passed out yet, and wasn't that proof that I still had work to do?

I asked Elliott if he'd ever been to the Bull Creek Flea Market.

Why don't you try and just rest, he said, except I had to keep murmuring—it was so much better than just sitting there in pain, to line up the words about the day I came across Agnes Martin's grids at Bull Creek in a big coffee table art book I'd found for four bucks. I'd had no idea she'd gotten herself down in words as precise and uncompromising as her strokes of color. I came across her *Writings* in a stack of water-stained cookbooks and war histories. The stack had been left to the side of the illustrated rifle books that all the flea vendors laid out front and center.

How Agnes ended up in that random stack of book detritus, I can't imagine. Half the pages were in German. Still, I'd found her. Waiting there, relegated to the haphazard pile on the table edge.

On the periphery is where it's at, I talked at Elliott. You want to see who's takin' a genuine risk, you got to look at the periphery. I rattled on, my throat so dry now I thought I might actually be talking myself to death. It's got to happen on the edge of something, I told him, something about to crumble, you know what I mean?

We were past the crest now and descending, the tree line starting to thin, bigger clumps of white and purple shithouse flowers taking over the roadside amid the dandelions.

And then at last there was Hamillville below, with its empty mill yards and brick buildings, same faded Bethlehem Steel sign languishing along the same river that moved through the emptiness of Sevlick on the other side of the ridge.

I told you we'd make it, I croaked, and Elliott shook his head, his hands still clenching the steering wheel.

After the first stoplight, we passed the block-long stretch of Rosen's department store, where my mother had bought her one good pair of shoes each year until it closed.

I gave Elliott a break from my frothing nonsense as he drove through the last two empty intersections before the hospital. He did handle the brakes better now, pulling into the emergency entrance and parking the truck just fine along the curb. Neither of us spoke as he lifted me once more into his arms. I reached for his neck but gave up. I was just too limp, couldn't steady my own neck as he carried me inside.

At the number of heads that turned when we entered the automatic doors, I felt Elliott's hand tense under my thigh. An older nurse in white pants blasted toward us, shouting for a gurney. Amid the sudden rush of sounds, the clicking straps and swishing doors, everything that had been said in the truck felt immediately irretrievable.

I'll wait out here, Elliott said as he backed away, and the older nurse pushing the gurney murmured that I'd raised a nice young man and wasn't that awfully hard to do.

Between the bolts of pain and my ever more delirious, horizontal state, it felt easier, once again, to clarify nothing and turn inward to Agnes. *My interest is in experience that is wordless and silent . . . to see ourselves in what we have received . . .*

LEAH

I've somehow miscalculated. It appears that I've trapped my family in a loop. We're coming down the wrong road for the second time and our tank's nearly empty. These forbidding hills are the last place I want to end up stalled on the roadside, exposed to whoever rolls up next. I'd fervently prefer a fairy tale for my stepmother that doesn't require my own death, in the belly of a wolf.

The gas light's blinking now on the dashboard, and we're at a corner we passed already, with a small brick house surrounded by large flags. We've passed a number of small houses with large flags on this loop we're stuck in, although this is the only house selling rabbits. On the front lawn, they're hopping about in a pen under a handwritten sign that says LIVE RABBITS $10. Silvestre spotted the pen through the window on our first time passing the house and begged to stop and pet the bunnies. He didn't want to hear about the nostalgic slogan on their flag, or my concern about the owners, how they might respond to us if we got out of the car and approached the pen.

Silvestre doesn't ask about petting the bunnies on our second time coming by this corner. He's too busy crying and I'd like to join him, to howl my head off. The arrow on my phone says the nearest gas station is still fifteen miles away. On the dashboard, the red blinking light feels like a rebuke of my delusions, conjuring a fairy tale for Jean instead of paying attention to the gas needle.

Gerardo and I both should've been keeping a closer eye. I should've taken a photo of the directions, should have remembered how little cell service there was in this area. And now our engine's begun to make a straining sound moving up a hill past a vacant strip mall with an abandoned Blockbuster and a closed laundromat. The Dollar Bargain looks like it might be open, or at least it has some kind of dim light inside.

We could stop somewhere along here, I suggest and Gerardo shrugs, says maybe at the chicken wing place coming up on the left, which has two cars out front.

Then we both spot it—a gas station at last, with the largest flags we've seen yet. We pull in anyhow, exchange no comments about the political slogans on the flags. We're too relieved and grateful for the prospect of gasoline, of being able to purchase as much of it as our rental tank will allow.

We pull into the open spot behind a young man in camo shorts. He's filling up an old station wagon rounded on the sides like the hull of a canoe. He looks about twenty or so, and the way he's turned and begun to steadily watch us makes me anxious. I resent his brazen stare as I unbuckle Silvestre and murmur to him in Spanish about having Velcroed his sneakers onto the wrong feet again. By the time I reverse Silvestre's shoes, the young man in the camo shorts has climbed back into his station wagon. At the sound of his engine catching, I reach down for Silvestre's hand, hold it tightly as we cross the lot to the bathroom, where we pass another man in camo shorts and also a matching camo vest. He has an immense eagle in the colors of the American flag inked onto his arm and I tense again, feeling absurd at how immediately my body stiffens in reaction to these young men. I recognize that I'll likely have a breakdown before we reach Jean's house if I panic about every man in this area who wears camo and stares at my family.

Just watch where you step, it's fine, I assure my son as I guide him around the wet globs of toilet paper on the bathroom floor. In the confines of the little stall, I flip up the toilet seat with my foot, help Silvestre position himself at the right distance from the stained edge of the bowl. It's a relief to give myself over to the clear procedure of these physical tasks, extracting soap from the broken dispenser, exiting without touching the handle on the door. Once we emerge, it occurs to me how rarely I've taken Silvestre into a bathroom that dirty, what a clean circle of existence I've maintained for him, so at odds with my years here with Jean, tagging along to her flea markets, holding my breath in the smelly porta-johns.

At the gas pumps, someone else has pulled in next to our rental car. There's now a silver truck with oversize wheels, an older woman who's addressing Gerardo. I see something tighten in the set of his mouth and recognize a tightness, too, in the grip of his fingers on the gas nozzle.

At the sight of the stickers on the back window of the woman's truck, I grab hold of Silvestre's small hand again, hurry him back across the parking lot, craning my neck to see the older woman at the other pump. She looks like she's in her late fifties or early sixties, though I can't see her face well under the brim of her stiff red cap, just the hunk of her gray hair in a ponytail. She's wearing a flannel shirt with the sleeves cut off at the shoulder, exposing her pale freckled arms, the skin above her elbows loose with age. When I rush up, Gerardo's nodding stiffly, saying he appreciates the input.

You better appreciate it, the woman at the other pump says.

In my alarm, I just stand there, clutching Silvestre's hand, and stare at the woman's bare arms, which are strong-looking for her age, same as Jean's when I saw her last. Behind her, the fuel numbers are rising so fast the flip of the digits has become dizzying.

Gerardo asks me in Spanish to get Silvestre into the car and I open the door.

The woman at the other pump asks why we don't talk in English. I don't tell her that I was born thirty miles from here or that my husband is a linguist who speaks four languages in addition to English. I attempt to restrain myself with another calming spell of physical tasks, adjusting the straps over Silvestre, buckling him up once more, brushing his shaggy brown hair out of his face.

Behind me, the woman repeats her question in a louder, more demanding voice. Why can't yins talk in English, she asks, like everybody else? She reminds us of the full name of the country, as if reciting the full name is indisputable evidence of something, though she doesn't state exactly what.

Once I shut Silvestre's door, I turn around, intending to end this encounter with dry understatement and composure, to resist blurring any aspects of this woman's contrarian energy with my stepmother. I swallow to stay calm, explain to her that we all speak English quite well but don't need to speak it for her sake.

Oh, you're one of them girls, aren't you? the woman at the other pump says, adjusting her red cap, revealing the underside of her bare freckled arm. I knew you were one of 'em, she says, I saw you strut out of the bathroom with your little half-breed and I knew it.

Behind me, Gerardo murmurs in Spanish that the tank's nearly full if I want to just get in the car, and I recognize in my mind that getting in the car right now would be an excellent choice. Except this woman's disgust for me has such a petrifying quality that I can't look away.

And it all surges up once more, the intensity and viciousness of my fight with Jean in her truck four years ago. A feeling like acid moves up my throat, a rise of bile I have to release.

You don't know shit about me! I shout. You don't know that I keep a hatchet in my trunk, I tell her, and you know what I like to do with it? I like to cut up racist bitches at gas stations and eat them for dinner!

The words gush out, too sour to swallow back down. At the other pump, the woman pulls in her face with surprise, causing the thin folds of loose skin under her chin to ripple. She begins to stroke the nozzle on her gas pump in a manner I can't look away from either. It's so odd and obscene. Why is she stroking her gas nozzle? And why did I just lie about a hatchet in my trunk?

Until Gerardo takes gentle hold of my arm, I don't realize I'm straining my neck, leaning forward to stare at her more ferociously.

In Spanish, Gerardo reminds me that Silvestre is in the car, and I find the restraint to keep my mouth closed. I ask Gerardo to take over the driving as the woman starts a new tirade, gripping her nozzle with both hands, shouting that I'm fuckin' nuts.

I flick her off, I can't resist, while making my silent way around the front of our rental car, aware of her gaze like a blast of foul air on my back.

Once I sink into the passenger's seat, I press the heels of my palms over my face, press down over my eye sockets until they ache. As soon as Gerardo gets in the car, I apologize. He asks what came over me and I tell him I don't know. So much for repeating Jean's name. So much for quietly conjuring a fairy tale for my stepmother, attempting to parse my grieving into scenes that add up to some kind of sense, instead of a madness of heartbreak arriving all at once—at a gas station.

Gerardo is kind enough not to comment. He turns over the engine, pulls out between the wildly flapping flags.

In the back seat, Silvestre asks what just happened, his voice high-pitched with bewilderment, and I don't know what to tell him. What kind of mother shouts at a stranger while pumping gas? I've just done the exact opposite of what I've dutifully instructed my child to do if somebody has an outburst on the playground.

I got everything wrong with that woman, I tell Silvestre. I let that woman suck me down with her and now I feel abysmal, I tell him, because that's not how I want to talk to anyone. Ever.

Silvestre blinks at this response under the cover of his long lashes. The quiet scrutiny on his small face is so excruciating I flip around to face the windshield instead, stare at the chicken wing place ahead of us once more, and it occurs to me that we don't have to continue this trip to see Jean's towers. I don't want to risk my son seeing me react that way to anyone else.

Maybe we should turn around, I suggest. We don't have to go through with this.

I tell them I'm not quite ready to step into Jean's house with some man living there I've never met. With Silvestre listening, I don't say how afraid I am that it might not be safe to go inside with Elliott, that anything at all could've happened to her in that house with him.

But we're nearly there, Gerardo says. He reminds me that I've been crying about Jean every night since Elliott called two weeks ago.

We have no idea what he'll be like, I say again, reminding Gerardo that we don't know anything about this man.

Gerardo insists Jean's housemate will probably be fine. He points out that Elliott was honest enough to call about my being in Jean's will and had been open-minded enough to help Jean make these towers, which seems pretty remarkable in a rural place like this, and worth seeing.

Silvestre, what do you think? Gerardo asks. You don't want to turn around, do you? This is his inheritance, too, he adds.

Of course it is, I agree, and also yours. It's just . . . not the right time to come here.

But when would the right time be? Gerardo asks, and having no answer for him, frantic to turn around for any reason at all, I tell him Jean couldn't have really cared about my seeing these towers. If she did, she could've written. She could've emailed pictures.

We should head back to State College, I say, or to Lancaster. I offer to find us a bed-and-breakfast. I tap my phone and start searching for options, decide the first one is perfect—a farm stay with pony rides, highly rated by 235 strangers.

But we've driven all this way, Gerardo says. Let's just go and see what happens. We could always make a quick stop, he adds, raising his eyebrows the way he often does before suggesting something outrageous. If it would put you at ease, he says, we can find a hardware store and buy a hatchet.

I laugh and reach for his hand. We're passing another stretch of small houses with large flags, all flapping with the same slogan, and I hope Gerardo won't regret his goodwill on this trip—or who he chose to marry. Who knows how many volatile particles of Jean may be drifting right now into my psyche, or maybe were latent in there already and have now been stirred up by her death?

Faster than I expected, we reach the first sign for the tiny town where I was born and that died long before Jean did. I squeeze my hands between my knees at the sight of its bland name that I rarely mention to anyone, and admit to Gerardo that he's absolutely right. Whatever attempt at artistic creation Jean managed to weld together here, I do want to see it. I also want my family to walk out of her house unharmed. For the sake of this brief tale, maybe Elliott doesn't have to be a figure out of "The Robber Bridegroom," with its cartoonish homicidal crew, and Jean doesn't have to be the eerie old woman in that story who stands by, watching, while the Robber Bridegroom and his crew find pleasure in dragging more victims inside and tossing them into a boiling pot.

Jean delighted in the horror of that tale, and I did, too. She read it to me often enough that I still remember that lone old woman who remains in the house where the men bring their victims. Although it's only now, with Jean dead, reaching this familiar sign, that it strikes me as curious that the tale provides no explanation for what keeps the old woman from attempting to leave, what compels her to stay there, coexisting with a pack of murderers. If she could help that young bride escape, why doesn't the old woman try to save herself, leave in the night as well?

And the tale, at least as I remember it, doesn't address what happens to the young bride after she escapes, whether she feels any pull to return to that grim house, any compulsion to know what happened to the old woman who crept out from behind the massive boiling pot and urged her to run.

JEAN

I got eighteen stitches, twelve internal and six along the skin. The stitches on the inside, the nurse said, would dissolve eventually, as most things under the skin are expected to do. Except, of course, for what the body doesn't know how to dissolve. Nitrates. Tar. Longing for a beloved child, her happy chatter absent in the morning and still absent in the evening. And no dissolving the strange black hole that is artistic inclination either, the weird inexplicable suck of it. I would have had a far easier life if I'd been satisfied with planting tulips or painting birdhouses. But the impulse had become the strongest thing in me, my compulsion to keep mangling with the dimensions of a box, the shape of the darkness inside it, the new secrets I could trap in the capsules on its sides. Why did the need to weld something totally useless become the only thing I craved to do with my days?

My stupidity with the grinder ruptured a whole slew of surface veins in my thigh. But you got pretty lucky, the attending doctor said while administering my tetanus shot. He told me the gash hadn't gone deep enough to bust an artery.

I'd think at your age, the doctor continued, it would be better to leave the heavy power tools alone, don't you agree? He raised his eyebrows as if warning an unruly child. His bald head was shiny and narrow as a bowling pin and I didn't see any need to agree. I just thanked him for the stitches and explained I had someone waiting to drive me home who couldn't stay much longer.

I hope you've got someone who can help when you get home, Mrs. Kovaseck. Is that how you say your name? he asked but didn't allow a pause for a reply before rushing into his instructions for the iron supplements I needed to take for the blood loss and his description of the sort of swelling or pus that would indicate an infection.

You really don't want those stitches to open, he warned. I know how expensive house repairs are but whatever you were trying to fix yourself, you really need to find a handyman now. We clear on that, Mrs. Kova-something?

I promised him it was clear to me as bird shit on a windshield. A young male nurse with tattooed arms and a tired face appeared. He wheeled me out to Elliott, who'd assumed the same position in the waiting room as on his front porch, his bony knees spread, hands clutching the phone between his legs as if it were the dashboard to the world.

I noticed Elliott's arms were no longer streaked with blood. He must have cleaned up in the hospital bathroom while he was waiting, had likely gone to wash off the blood as soon as he was rid of me. There was nothing to be done, though, about the now ferrous-colored splotches of dried blood on his shirt and down the front of his baggy carpenter jeans.

I apologized for how long he'd had to sit and wait, and he told me it was all right. The sour odor of his body felt familiar now, as he leaned over to help me out of the wheelchair and onto the crutches. At the contact of his hands against my rib cage, I felt an unexpected surge of relief and grabbed his shoulder.

You all right? he asked and I nodded, the ache radiating down my leg too overwhelming for me to speak. It was already five p.m. by then and I hadn't eaten since breakfast. I realized Elliott must be ravenous as well. Once he got me settled, he secured the crutches on loan from the hospital in the truck bed and climbed into the cabin. I asked if he was hungry, if maybe he wanted to stop at the McDonald's drive-through down the block before heading back over the ridge to Sevlick.

Hell, yes, he said.

At the red light, a bent and broken-looking man crossed in front of us with a shopping cart full of soda cans. The man had two kids with him, both with the same reddish hair and struggling to lug a long, heavy duffel bag between them.

I bet they've got the mother in that bag, I said to Elliott and he snorted.

You've got a dark fuckin' mind, he said.

Oh you bet I do, I told him. What do you think all those crazy boxes are about? I keep trying to get all the darkness into them, but my mind just keeps makin' more. It's the damnedest thing.

I liked the relaxed half smile on Elliott's face at this response as the light changed and we drove on toward the McDonald's. It felt awfully good to be sealed again into the truck cabin together, to be not dead after all—and not alone, to be taking in the sad trickle of humanity left in Hamillville with him. Nobody would have ever found out, or cared, if he'd walked out of my house and left me bleeding to death next to the workbench. He was clearly attuned enough to pick up on the sonar of my total solitude, to recognize the unlikelihood of anyone caring how I expired. He could have walked out with my wallet. Or he could've been human enough to get the rag and help with the tourniquet, but refused to drive the truck.

And yet here we were, getting on just fine—my leg stitched up, the two of us waiting for fries and milkshakes at the Hamillville McDonald's. *At every moment we are presented with happiness, with the sublime,* Martin said, a mantra that felt fleetingly more possible waiting with Elliott outside the drive-through window despite the defunct Denny's and empty candy store across the street, despite the postmortem torpor all around us.

I'm grateful to you, Hounslow, I really am, I said as we waited for our bag of dinner. And you know what, I told him, I believe you're on the holy squad now of people who've saved an old lady.

Elliott gave a faint shake of his head at this, his lips pressed together, and I told him I hoped I hadn't made him too uncomfortable with all my pompous ranting on the way to the hospital.

With his face still turned toward the pickup window, he murmured that he hadn't minded. At least, he said, you have somethin' you give a shit about.

I do have that, I agreed, too moved by his answer to think of anything more to say.

You know, I said at last, you're an unusually mild man, Hounslow. I sure hope you're able to stay that way.

Doubt it, he said as the takeout window finally slid open and he reached toward the woman at the window, who looked about my age. She had a long yellowish bruise on the saggy arm she extended with our cardboard drink tray and our bag of dinner.

I hope yins have a real blessed day, she said with such a bleak forced smile I couldn't bear it. I murmured to Elliott to press on the gas and get us the hell out of there, and he did, packing fries into his mouth, chewing them up with such verve and pleasure, driving back down the road past the hospital. I couldn't look away from his busy, vigorous mouth, that scar moving in his lower lip as he ate. It was rejuvenating to watch him, his pimple-pocked, broad cheeks working on each bite, his bitten-down fingernails pinching the bun on his Big Mac and lifting it to his mouth. I felt immediately more alive myself, taking in all the spooled-up youth and hunger Elliott still had wound inside him.

The softening light as we started back up the ridge felt like a seduction, too, the evening creeping into the trees. The first purplish shadows were already rising up through the forest, taking over the mossy rocks and scaling the branches, greedy and eating up the light. To drive through these ancient trees at the end of the day widened the mind, opened some creaky gate in there.

God, I love this creepy hour, don't you? I said and Elliott gave one of his barely perceptible nods in response, took a loud sip of his Coke.

I tried to get a job doing road work up here, he said.

Is that right? And what happened? I asked.

They said they couldn't take me, he said. I got in the wrong fuckin' car two years ago.

I asked what kind of wrong and he said stolen, drugs in the trunk, and took the next turn around the mountain too sharply.

I didn't know anyone in the car 'cept my neighbor, he went on, fisting his hands around the wheel. The pigs who pulled us over really scored.

I told him I was sorry and waited for him to elaborate on what kind of record had come of it, if that arrest with his neighbor was the reason he never left the house now, but Elliott just reached for his Coke and I didn't press him. None of my business if that was the whole story or not, and he had more than earned my trust, delivering me alive to Hamillville. It felt right and fair for him to get something out of this time in the truck, too—to tell whatever version of himself felt true and worth saying aloud now, driving over a mountain with a stranger, the dusk clipping at the tips of the trees.

When Elliott bent forward to eat the last of his fries, I saw he still had a smear of my blood on the back of his neck and I told him.

You're welcome to use my shower when we get back, I offered. Seems the least I can do.

He stiffened and I didn't push him to answer. We were already descending into Sevlick by then, fast approaching the absolute nothing that awaited us both on Paton Street.

When Elliott pulled into the driveway, I asked if he would mind helping me into the house. Just into the door would be a huge help, I said as if there were a need to convince him. As if he had much of a choice.

His lack of choice felt undeniable as we pulled up in front of our two homes. My house wasn't in great shape, but at least the roof was intact and all the floorboards on the porch were in place. The house Elliott's family was renting had been a good-looking house at one point. The D'ercoles had kept the shutters painted a bright white against the pewter gray the house was painted then. After Peggy D'ercole died and a string of renters wore the house down, her son stopped bothering with any up-keep. He died of liver problems in Florida and the same bank in West Virginia that had bought all the other foreclosed houses here in the East End bought it up.

By the time Elliott and his family moved in, there were no shutters left and half the floorboards on the front porch were torn up or missing, the cracks in the front windows patched with masking tape. Of course, none of us still owning on Paton Street bothered with repainting anything either. Nobody wanted to draw any unnecessary attention with a new paint job, looking like they had money to spare.

For now, just having energy to spare, enough to reach the front door, seemed daunting. I felt dizzy getting out of the truck. It was an effort to stay vertical. Even with the painkillers, an ache burned up my leg, hot as a welding rod. I felt like cinder by the time we entered the front room. Next to the band saw, I paused to get my bearings, take in the miracle that I was back among my Manglements. All their dented lids I'd banged out of shape intentionally. All the demented determination that had gone into welding the capsules bulging on their sides. Seeing them again, dizzy, but not dead, was hypnotizing—the tilting sides of the boxes, the angle varied each time, same as I had the contents of the capsules. I spotted the silver boat and penguin from an old Monopoly game I'd picked up for fifty cents, the creepy little soldiers I'd found last summer in a toy war set.

Odd how I can't stop making these things, isn't it? I said and Elliott laughed.

You'll get back to 'em, whatever the hell they are, he replied.

I call them Manglements, I told him. Elliott nodded at this divulgence, made no comment as he helped me maneuver my crutches past the workbench. After all this time keeping that nonsense name to myself, the sound of it aloud in front of Elliott upped the dizziness in my head. And yet it felt good, too, awfully good—risking the name aloud while I crutched forward another step, and then forward again. Self-repeating, self-unafraid, self-trusting . . . Louise had a whole list of self-requisites that made art seem like something any obsessive loner who craved it could achieve. Although what if deep down, where the art should be, there was just a fearful homebody, just a nervous tinkerer?

Jesus, this hurts like hell, I muttered, leaning more on Elliott as we got past the workbench. You can dump me on the sofa, I told him, trying not to grunt, to crutch a little faster down the hall into the den.

Want me to carry you? he offered and I said he didn't have to, although once we passed the kitchen, his grip under my arms was all that kept me upright until I collapsed onto the sunken beige couch in the TV den. Without asking, he helped me inch forward to a more comfortable position and readjusted the lumpy throw pillow behind my head. I'd meant to replace those beaten-up pillows my father had thrown all the time. He'd chucked them at people on the news who annoyed him.

Elliott's subdued presence was such a welcome contrast to the endless agitation I associated with that TV den. After murmuring my thanks, I offered him the shower again and he lowered his face, stuffed his hands down into the deep front pockets of his carpenter jeans. I thought he was going to give one of his polite nods and leave, to give primacy to his pride and deny his clear need of a good scrubbing with soap and water.

I was wrong so often about Elliott. Except, I suppose, when I happened to guess right.

His voice soft, barely audible, he murmured okay and I restrained myself from saying anything more as he shuffled out of the den toward the bathroom.

Once he shut the door behind him, I let my head fall back against the sofa. The exhaustion I'd been denying gave way through my body like a mudslide. I thought of my father's second-to-last morning on this couch, when he admitted he could have just kept his mouth shut at the scrapyard and we would've been better off. They weren't the worst Jews, he said of his in-laws, you know what I mean? Sure, I told him, though I'd barely gotten to know my mother's parents given how rabidly my father loathed them. I'd planned to replace this couch as soon as he died. Except I went out and bought my Grizzly band saw instead, then blew a bunch of money on a plasma cutter and new parts for my welder.

Half-conscious on the couch, it didn't occur to me until I heard the shower start that Elliott had nothing to dry off with except the two navy-blue hand towels on the rack next to the sink. With him already under the water, it seemed too late to shout about getting a bath towel from the closet upstairs, and I was in no shape to go up and get one for him.

I wondered if he had already realized this problem of the towel as well, if he was thinking about it as the water ran over his chest and on down between his legs. Motionless on the sofa, I felt like no more than a sack of failing cells. Just a floating, lonely mind picturing Elliott naked in my shower, reaching for the old soap in the corner.

It felt harmless enough to go on imagining him in there once the water stopped. I guessed he must be rubbing himself dry with one of the worn blue hand towels. Unless he was trying to dry off with his T-shirt instead. Something metal clinked in the bathroom against what sounded like porcelain. The button on his jeans, I imagined, against the toilet, and with a rush of pleasure I pictured him tugging those unwashed jeans of his up over his bony ass, pushing the metal button through its hole.

At the creak of the bathroom door, I blushed, although all I'd done was indulge in a few lewd thoughts. Nothing men didn't do in every bar all over the world every night. I was an old nobody stuck on her parents' sofa after grinding into her own leg. What did it matter what went through my mind? It was astounding I was alive at all. And so wild that Elliott was the reason.

A minute later, he appeared in the doorway, his pale forehead still pink from the shower, his broad cheeks splotchy. He said nothing about the lack of bath towels or how he'd made do without one, and I didn't ask. I just stared at the size of the rust-brown blood smears on his Steelers shirt and down the front of his loose jeans.

There's no way in hell those stains are going to wash out, I said. Let me give you some cash to replace 'em.

Elliott backed up immediately into the doorway and mumbled that it was all right, he had other clothes.

You sure you're okay getting around? he asked as he receded farther, already retreating from my cluttered den.

I said of course, no need at all to worry about me.

accurate in describing thought processing in other people's minds.

LEAH

On the exit ramp, we pass a billboard for John Deere tractors and Jean's homemade card comes back to me. She mailed it my first year in college, for my birthday, and I threw it away immediately. She'd covered the front of the card with a creepy collage, circles of random things cut out of magazine ads. John Deere tractor wheels had formed half the circles, with women in high-rise cotton underwear forming the other half, alongside cutouts of people's mouths, smiling in ads for Tic Tacs.

For Jean to make a collage that bizarre and crass with me in mind, and for my first birthday on my own in college, was so bewildering I didn't just throw it away. I hid it beneath various disposable coffee cups in the dorm garbage can, frantic to eliminate any chance of my roommates spotting that creepy mix of tractor parts and women's crotches. I didn't want to find out if I could make a joke about Jean's card to my roommates without crying.

As soon as I'd had an address at college, I'd sent it to Jean, hoping we could reconnect now that I was living on my own terms and not my father's. When that envelope from her arrived,

I anticipated a funny store-bought birthday card with something loving written inside, something maternal. It was Jean who told me that the original Grimm fairy tales made no divide between mothers who gave birth to their children and the mothers devoted to offspring who entered their lives some other way. I knew Jean had moved out because she was fed up with my father, and yet she had never acknowledged, even obliquely, on the phone or in a letter, that I was the loss she'd been willing to assume in order to get away from him.

Instead, she'd made me a collage of tractor parts and crotch shots. Inside the card, she'd written nothing but *Keep rollin', kiddo! Love ya.* Until receiving this jokey single line from Jean, I hadn't recognized how much I was longing, that first year in college, for steady maternal assurance. I wanted what my roommates received from their mothers, store-bought cards with cursive fonts and affirming messages about the joy of having a daughter.

After Jean's crotch-and-tractor card arrived, I got disoriented on my way to class, unsure if I was in the right building. I had to recheck the number on the door to make certain I wasn't about to humiliate myself and take a seat at the wrong seminar table. My bouts of disorientation got so bad I went to see a counselor in student services, who reassured me that it was reasonable to cut Jean out of my life for a year or two, at least until I could reach a classroom without halting in panic.

The same counselor told me she knew of other motherless students like me, who would strain to hear what their roommates said on the phone when they spoke to what sounded like involved, reassuring mothers. She said those students would listen to their roommates on the phone the same way I did, eavesdropping like people hoping to develop an ear for a language they'd been yearning to grasp for years. Some of these motherless eavesdroppers, she told me, became adept at acquiring other languages instead. She told me that focusing on a new syntax of any kind could become an escape hatch into new habits of mind, and I believed her. I applied for post-college jobs beyond the English-speaking world and moved to Peru three weeks after graduation.

When I saw Jean four years ago, it was after living with Gerardo in Lima for a decade. A hemisphere away from the Allegheny Mountains, everything I'd lived early and in English receded beneath the rising tide of my days in Spanish. If anyone asked about my childhood, I gave a vague summary as if my life had begun at age ten, sweeping Jean out of the tale entirely, which felt sneaky but acceptable. Or so I told myself, as once sneakiness feels acceptable, it's hard not to get carried away. At a party a few months ago with some parents in Silvestre's bilingual preschool, the subject of the Rust Belt came up, and I rolled my eyes, said that social progress in this country would happen much faster once everyone in those failing towns who was white and over the age of sixty had died. I felt uneasy even as I said it, and I didn't sleep well that night, wondering how Jean was doing, if she'd ever break down and send an email to say she was thinking of me, if it was cruel that I'd yet to tell her I'd had a child.

Last October, I scooped out all the stringy insides of a giant pumpkin for Silvestre onto the kitchen table the way Jean had done for me every Halloween. I thought of her as I took a video of Silvestre's gleeful delight, smearing the pumpkin innards across the tabletop and pressing the sticky seeds into his forehead. I longed to send Jean the video and would have, if I hadn't excluded her from the news of his birth and every milestone since.

My family and I have now driven off the exit ramp. We're well past the John Deere billboard, and Gerardo has flicked on the turn signal. I remember this stone church to the left of us, next to the now-closed library where Jean would always grab at least one random book from the returns cart and remind me of her belief in reading with serendipity.

After a block, we reach the plaza at the center of town. More of the benches look rotted or broken than I remember from four years ago, when I last returned here and saw Jean—a visit so painful and infuriating that I left resolved to erase her permanently, to avoid her influence on my marriage and the kind of mother I might become. I wanted a clean start with Gerardo and with our future children.

Why, then, do I feel utterly filthy now, as off-kilter as the tilting trash can on the corner, overflowing with broken stroller parts and pizza boxes? On the streets lining the plaza, every storefront is boarded over except for a run-down deli with a flashing red lottery sign in the window, casting a red glow over the stacked boxes of Marlboros beneath it.

Around the corner, some optimistic person is keeping a small café going with green picnic tables out front for whoever still lives here to find one another. For the moment, nobody seems to be finding company here. A spectral quiet reigns over the empty picnic tables and a rusted music stand holding a battered Sesame Street book I recognize, with Elmo and Grover dancing on the cover.

The attempt at vitality in this café is so strong I ask Gerardo to stop the car. Inside, on the plywood countertop, freshly baked pumpkin gobs have been piled into a pyramid, ringed with tiny plastic-wrapped peanut butter buckeyes, baked goods I haven't thought about in years. I'm overwhelmed with a desire for Silvestre and Gerardo to experience the whipped cream icing inside the gobs when they bite into them and the icing squishes out. I want Silvestre to enjoy the fun of licking all the pumpkin icing off his lips. The gobs and buckeyes are only a dollar each and I ask if I can buy them all and in two boxes, one for us and a second box for Elliott, as an offering, to help get through the awkwardness of meeting a stranger who's taken over my stepmother's house and perhaps is lying about her death.

I'm trying to keep my mind from fixating on that possibility of deceit, to concentrate instead on the pumpkin spice aroma of the just-baked gobs on my lap. We're now passing a house with boards nailed over every window and a large grim X spray-painted on the front door. Most of the houses on Jean's street have boarded-over windows or smashed glass. Some have no glass or plywood, just rectangular window-shaped holes opening onto abandoned rooms and darkness.

I hope there is still glass in Jean's windows when we arrive. With every pothole we hit on my stepmother's street, I feel the jolt of our total silence these past four years, the finality of it vibrating my jaw and every disk in my spine.

I can't recall how many blocks are left before we reach her house. When Jean lived with me and my father, we had a house on the other side of town, where the homes were larger and the school district had more money. I'd only come here with Jean every few weeks to check on her dad. He was always in the garage when we came to see him and he wouldn't turn off the awful growling sounds of his tools when we arrived. He was a small man, shorter and slighter than my own father, and far older, and yet I found him terrifying. He'd never look at me straight on or open the garage door. The dimness inside had the damp closed-off energy of a cave. On the floor, he used emptied soup cans to hold things—various assortments of screws, nails, and sawed-off bits of sheet metal that never seemed to change. If Jean's father ever knelt and looked at what he'd accumulated in those tin cans, I never saw it happen. A rusted fire pail on the floor contained a mess of bigger, more jagged steel shards and empty Altoid tins.

Do you think you could stop being a bastard and say hello? Jean shouted at her father every visit over the incessant noise of his tools. Don't you want to say hello to my Leah?

I see her, she's a fine girl, Jean's father would reply, giving me a nod at most, but never the direct hello that Jean demanded of him. I couldn't understand why she sought this same futile battle with him every time.

Git me that other drill bit, Jeanie, her father would command, and she would oblige, at first. Sometimes he'd order her to do two or three things and I would cower by the steps, waiting. Jean knew all his tools. She never needed him to specify what he was talking about. He made gate hinges for people, and lumber racks for the backs of trucks, and he repaired things, too, something with a metal knob on top he called a tow hitch. Whatever he was working on, Jean would urge him to add a flourish that he didn't want to add, a decorative twist to a hinge, or a contrast in the metals.

C'mon, Dad, she'd tell him. You have all these weird alloys, mix it up for once, or let me do it.

Lay off, Jeanie, he'd warn her. Nobody wants any girlie bullshit. They just want a rack like everyone else.

You know you want to mix it up, though, she'd taunt him and eye me. Once she gave me that silent warning, I'd get a sick feeling, knowing what was coming next. She was going to hand her dad something other than what he asked of her. A different type of bit or disk, or another grimy tool entirely. There was a metal stool her father had made and kept in the garage, and Jean liked to kick the legs, tell him he should weld on some washers, make the legs look like the suckers on an octopus. This stool's just sitting in here, it'll be fun, Dad, why the hell not?

That's enough, Jeanie. Take your girl and git goin', he'd warn, though we never left then. Not before Jean let out one of her gulping laughs and he threw a work glove at her, or one of the Altoid tins, and she'd hurl something back. I didn't understand why she wanted to stay, to keep pushing closer to the possibility that they might kill each other.

Jean, please, let's go, I pleaded with her every time, same as I did that night on the cliff four years ago. But once she got their duel going, she couldn't extract herself, not until she provoked her father a bit more, poked a little harder at some truth about his unused creative impulses and her own that neither of them acknowledged except when they went after each other in the most primordial way. Maybe those battles in the garage allowed them to release something neither had figured out how to release otherwise.

Once, Jean hit her father on the neck with a little piece of metal and he whipped around with such rage, there was a bulging in his face. He called her a little bitch and Jean kicked his steel workbench hard enough to send the tools and loose pieces of metal on top of it clanging to the floor. Her father threw a handful of nails at her in response, the ding of them against the floor echoing in the chamber of the closed garage. I did my best to flatten myself against the wall, waiting for Jean to remember I was there, for her instinct to get us out of that garage unharmed to overcome her hunger to rile up her father just a little more.

I didn't wait for Jean that visit. When her father grabbed a second handful of nails, I scrambled up the garage steps to reach the door into the house, hoping Jean had gotten enough of whatever she needed from him and we could escape.

Bye, Dad, great to see you! she shouted, cackling and grabbing my arm, pulling me after her into the kitchen, where her father never followed us. She didn't let go of her hold on my arm until the front door banged shut behind us and we were released into the daylight on the porch, which even in winter felt reassuring and bright after being trapped in the damp cave of that garage with her father.

You know what's going to be beautiful, she said as we pulled out of the driveway. What's going to be beautiful is when that bastard is good and dead and I get his precious welder for myself. Oh, I've got so many ideas, Leah, she told me. I could bury that bastard in all the ideas I have that he wouldn't dare consider. I'd go right now and get my own welder, she added, but your dad would hate the noise. He'd go nuts about the mess. He wouldn't let up until he sucked all the fun out of it.

When Jean rambled this way in the car, she didn't pause for me to respond. More than a year passed before she left us. Maybe two years. I never considered whether she'd actually start to weld and what she'd make. I'm trying to prepare myself for the possibility that her towers will be a little pitiful and clumsy. I don't know what I'll do if something about them is beautiful, if I'm so clouded with grieving that I can't take them in on their own, apart from this dying town that Jean never had the audacity to leave, though she had the audacity to leave me.

You got pretty lucky, she'd say whenever we reread "Hansel and Gretel." I'd never abandon you in the woods, she'd tell me, just to gobble up your dinner myself. I'd only forget you in the forest, she'd joke, if there was something special going on.

Four years ago, on my last visit here, a group of men showed up next to us in the forest and Jean immediately turned her back to me. When I got frantic to leave, she laughed as if my desire to get away from those men was baseless, nothing but snobbery. She stuck by them until the sun was down to a sliver and they could have done anything at all to us, deep in the woods of these sinking mountains, with the dark coming on.

JEAN

If Elliott had no desire to speak to me again, he could have avoided it. He could have asked his mother to come give a courtesy knock the next morning. He could have sent his sister, too, to check in and make sure I hadn't tumbled on the crutches and turned into a corpse. He could have sent no emissary at all. The two of us could have gone back to politely nodding at each other, pretending I didn't know what his bony chest felt like against the side of my head. We could have pretended he had no idea about the excellent water pressure in my shower.

Except Elliott didn't go with any of those options. He came himself—and at eleven, well after his sister had left for school and his mother headed up the hill for more drudgery at the deli.

I didn't hear his knock from all the way back in the den, where I'd slept on the sofa. I hadn't bothered to try changing my clothes yet. Just getting to the bathroom was effort enough. I hadn't expected to do anything but exist with my leg up, watching Fellini movies and flipping through the Van Gogh biography I'd found at the flea market months ago and that had been waiting on the coffee table since then. I'd watched the morning news for a few minutes until I remembered why I was more content when I skipped it. No president or party that took over Washington ever did much for Paton Street. The number of gunshots and boarded-over windows seemed to go up every year regardless of who slept in the White House.

I clicked the remote to find some voices from any era that was not this one, when instead I heard a voice much closer.

Jean? Um . . . Mrs. Kovasevic? Elliott's hesitant call through the door plucked me back to the present.

Coming, hold on, I yelled from the den. No matter how carefully I rose from the sofa, I couldn't avoid how painfully the skin still pulled around the stitches. My whole body felt like corroded metal, scaling and rusted through. I hobbled along on the crutches anyhow to the front door, so Elliott would know he didn't need to break in to check on me.

Nearly there, I shouted at a higher volume than necessary, although the robust sound of my vocal cords was reassuring. Until I swung the door open, I'd forgotten I was still in the same bloodstained, crumpled pants I'd been wearing yesterday. I pretended I didn't notice Elliott taking in my unchanged clothes, my hair hanging in gray hunks, half of it out of the gumband that was supposed to keep it all in a ponytail, my calloused feet bare against the floor.

Come on in, please, I said. Let me make you a cup of coffee.

I don't want to be a bother, Elliott said, stepping on the tip of one of his unlaced boots with the other. I just wanted to make sure you were doin' all right.

He looked past me into the living room then, ran his palm

over the dark stubble on his head, the splotches I knew to look for already creeping up his cheeks. He'd arrived in a clean pair of worn jeans, the same light blue wash as yesterday, but looser on him, baggy to the point of having lost their shape completely. His gray T-shirt was from Deicker's Shooting Range, the letters exploding from a large red bull's-eye on his chest.

So what'd your mom say, I asked, about my forcing you to drive me all the way over to Hamillville?

Elliott shrugged. What'd your daughter say? he asked.

My daughter? I repeated and then caught myself. Well Leah's no fool, I told him. She knows a lost cause like me doesn't die that easily.

C'mon in, I urged him, opening the door wider, motioning with one of my crutches for him to enter, which he did, stopping next to the thick sheets of scrap metal he'd brought in the day before. Elliott's expression was too withholding to guess why he'd paused, if it was to doubt how skilled I actually was with the tools in this room, or whether he was still interested in my teaching him to operate the grinder. I couldn't think of anything else to offer him, now that I had him in the house again.

So what do you think? I asked him. You want to take the grinder for a spin? You did just fine with my truck.

I don't want to slice my leg off, he said.

Oh, you won't, I told him. That only happened because the cord was tangled. You'll be fine, c'mon.

When he hesitated, I assured him I would stand next to the workbench and guide him, though I didn't know if I had the stamina to stay upright on the crutches. I felt sluggish just from the effort to get to the front door. I wasn't going to be able to stand much longer without painkillers.

Come on, I said, motioning to him. You might as well learn. It's a useful skill to pick up somewhere, don't you think?

Elliott shrugged, although he was openly eyeing the grinder now, and I didn't have to say anything else for him to shuffle a few feet closer. It felt as hushed as that hidden creek where I used to take Leah, our slow wade toward the workbench. Elliott brought in a kitchen chair for me to rest on and a second chair for me to elevate my leg. I thanked him and asked if maybe he could bring in the bag of Herr's barbecue chips, which I'd left next to the toaster.

It's a little early for chips, I told him, but I feel like it.

Not too early for me, Elliott said, already shuffling in his heavy boots toward the kitchen. We had no problem finishing the bag between us, sinking again into the familiarity we'd established yesterday. I pointed out the rag on the workbench where he could wipe the chip grease off his fingers before he handled the grinder. He operated it with far less clumsiness than he had the truck, owing, perhaps, to the fact that he was not distracted by my bleeding and writhing next to him. Properly bandaged now, wincing only occasionally, I guided him on what to do.

A little bit higher, I explained, lifting my arm to demonstrate how he needed to angle the buffing disk. Sitting off to the side, I felt like a conductor, gesturing in the air to show him how to unclamp the scrap of metal still fastened to the workbench from when I'd dropped the grinder yesterday.

You don't need to press down like that, I told him. You can let up a bit, just move the buffing disk along the surface. You don't need anything more than contact.

Elliott nodded. He tried again, but still didn't get the movement exactly right. I kept my mouth shut and let him keep trying, to reach the quiet pleasure of figuring out the angle for himself. It revived something in me just to watch him, his earnest focus, the hesitation in his attempts, his timid way of looking over at me. The sight of someone else in this room felt good, sharing the light coming in the window. The leather scraps under the workbench had soaked up the bloodstains from yesterday. The brownish blotches now looked like spots that could be from any number of spills, not necessarily a burst of blood from mishandling a grinder. Other drops had already dried and vanished into the floorboards. There was so little evidence of anything having gone horribly wrong, making it easy to lose sense of how much blood had come gushing out. The shock felt distant already, how close I'd come to becoming the next corpse discovered in a worthless house in the East End.

With nobody on the street talking much anymore, it felt easy to put the accident out of mind and tell myself it hadn't really been that big a deal, and that whatever happened next with Elliott wasn't a big deal either. The world wasn't paying attention to either of us. There seemed no reason to care what the hell anyone thought of the two of us tinkering in here together.

I don't know if it would interest you, I said, but I could pay you if you could help with the lifting again tomorrow. I could use an extra hand until my leg heals.

Elliott said nothing for a moment, maintaining his usual in-scrutable expression, and I wondered if I'd just embarrassed my-self, admitting so plainly my need for his help, and that I had the cash to pay for it.

You don't have to, I said. It was just an idea.

I don't mind, Elliott said with a shrug. I can do whatever you want.

He didn't ask what kind of pay I had in mind and I didn't specify. It felt easier to let the question go while Elliott went on buffing the rest of the first sheet and the sun began to heat up the front room. I showed him how to clamp the next heavy sheet to the workbench. I didn't want to break the good tempo we'd found, the welcome intimacy of being with someone else in this room. With the temperature rising, my skin started to sweat un-der the bandage, getting itchy around the incision.

I just need a minute, I told him, struggling to get myself verti-cal on the crutches, aware once more of Elliott observing me, taking in my crumpled, bloodstained clothes from yesterday.

I should probably get going, he said, and it was like the ceiling fell, the collapse I felt at his desire to leave.

All right, I said, go on, Hounslow. I'll see you tomorrow same time.

Once he'd gone, I passed out on the couch, dizzy with fatigue. I woke in the dark to shouts outside, a threat to blow somebody's head off. A car door banged, the sound close enough that if someone pulled a trigger, a stray bullet could come flying through my front window. I thought of Elliott and his family listening to the same shouts across the small strip of grass between us, all of us awake and waiting for whatever might come next.

I listened to the ultimatums, a second threat about killing somebody's mother, trying to gauge whether things were escalating out there. At last, a couple of car doors banged at once and it was over, no sound outside but the howl of Steve Pavlikowski's sad, cooped-up hound in the backyard it never got to leave.

I crutched my way into the hall bathroom to use the toilet. This kind of rabid shouting at night had been rare until the past ten years or so. This summer, it had struck me as especially unnerving. I was just getting tired of it—or getting old. Leaning on the sink edge, I let the water pour over my hands until it warmed, and I thought of Elliott next door, the nothing at all that would run from his family's faucet if any of them went into their bathroom right now, seeking some water to help get back to sleep. I couldn't imagine those four jugs lasted them until nighttime, unless they carefully rationed in order to have enough left to brush their teeth.

If Elliott did return in the morning, I would tell him he was welcome to fill the jugs more than once a day. Although maybe it would be too awkward to bring up his family's need of the spigot when we were working so closely. Yes, probably better to say nothing, avoid making him uneasy about coming here. I didn't want to come across as desperate for his help.

The next morning right at eleven, he arrived and for a moment, his tense, physical presence in the doorway caught me off guard. In the bathroom last night, worrying about him and his family waking up with no water to drink, I'd forgotten about his reluctance to say more than four words at once, about his buzzed head and slumped posture, the mask of blankness he'd been taught to wear, that sense that some kind of snake must be coiled in him, and it was only a matter of time before something I said, or did, would release it.

"Morning, Hounslow. Hear that racket last night?" I held the door open for him and he stepped inside, said yep, he'd heard all right and didn't care.

I'm used to it, he told me. Where we were staying for a while, he said, over in Fayette County was fuckin' worse.

Hard to think of Paton Street, I joked, as an improvement on anywhere.

Elliott said nothing in response, just lowered his face, and I wished I could take the joke back. I'd already popped two of the painkillers from the hospital by then and had revved up on coffee, to offset them. My mind was whirring at a crazy blend of slow and fast. I felt itchy this morning, too, and couldn't do anything about it. The nurse had told me I couldn't shower until tomorrow, could only wipe down with a damp towel, avoiding the stitches, which I'd done before Elliott arrived, and changed into one of my dad's old coveralls.

How about we get going then, you ready? I asked, churning up the brightness of my voice to turn things around. What would be great, I told him, would be to buff the rest of those sheets you carried in. You were a natural with the grinder yesterday, I added and was pleased to see Elliott cross right to the workbench, at ease enough in the room to do that. He went right ahead and

loosened the clamp, removed the sheet metal he'd finished buffing yesterday. He didn't seem to be bothered that I'd taken a seat
and was watching him intently. My father had hated for me to sit
and watch him work. He'd start to shout for me to fetch things
that he didn't need. I was the only kid on Paton Street with a
father who rarely left the garage and was too hotheaded to hold
a real job, who had a mother who worked at the pharmacy and
didn't pull in until six. The only way I'd been able to sit still and
observe my dad weld was to spy on him through the screen door
between the kitchen and the garage. It had felt like a game,
crouching there, knowing how furious he would get if he caught
me, hearing him murmur to himself under his helmet, watching
him add a little spiral to a bronze latch. If he risked a flourish,
he'd always grind it down later and leave no trace of it. He never
talked to himself in that subdued way inside the house, like he
was murmuring a prayer. It never occurred to me that the secret
release I saw him find under the cover of his helmet might be the
best gift he didn't intend to give me.

At my father's old workbench now, Elliott had found his
rhythm and looked like he was enjoying himself, re-clamping
the sheet metal to buff the rest.

It's fun, isn't it? I asked him. Working at the rust on something and seeing what happens?

Yeah, I guess, he said.

Oh c'mon, Hounslow, I urged him. It won't kill you to admit
something's enjoyable.

He smiled at this, and I wished I had the strength to get up
and teach him something more.

Even with the painkillers, I couldn't stand longer than a few minutes without wincing. The skin around the incision felt alarmingly tight today, like the stitches had shrunk overnight. I forced myself up anyhow and crutched my way to the workbench. The morning cool had just about passed, the room warming around us.

Elliott asked to open the windows and I said sure. The sunlight had gotten sharper, revealing the gradations of color in the sheet metal as he finished buffing the second sheet. None of the lifting seemed to cause him much strain, nothing compared to the effort all the lifting would have required of me. He worked with a youthful ease that was mesmerizing to watch. Even with the room heating up, he'd hardly broken a sweat, just a few drops trailing the sides of his broad, pale face.

Buffing the third piece of sheet metal, he let out a brief whistling sound, not a confident, robust sort of whistle. Elliott never allowed himself a confident, robust sound of any kind, or at least not in my presence, and it moved me, hearing him release that soft burst of whistling under his breath as he worked the rust off the third sheet. I didn't comment on it. While he buffed the rest, I marked the lines I'd figured out with a tar-paper model I'd made before the grinder accident. The idea for this new Manglement had come to me in bed, staring up at the sunken corner of the same ceiling I'd stared at my whole childhood. I'd never planned on waking there again, not when I left for college—and not after I left again, after marrying Dave. Growing old now, under that sunken corner, I had to do something with the shape

of it. To make a rectangular lid just warped enough to eliminate any possibility of ever closing the box completely felt just
right.

I didn't explain any of this to Elliott. Only that I thought this
new box could be a little bigger than the others, now that I had
his help with the lifting.

I've wanted to go bigger for a long time, I told him, although
I did not say forty years.

That tower there might be cool in a bigger size, he said, pointing at my narrowest Manglement on the floor near the band saw.
It was a good bit taller than the others, totem-like, and it had
something of that holy air about it that totemic shapes can have.

I think you're absolutely right, I told him. That tower shape
would be a hell of a lot cooler at five or six feet high.

I'd strained my shoulder maneuvering the longer sides of that
totem shape on my own. The two-feet-tall sides had been worth
the strain, though, for the extra surface area. I'd been able to
weld my tiny dioramas in a rising corkscrew over the four sides
like a spiral stairwell, which I'd never tried before. The photos
I'd glued into the capsules had a mix of women's feet and horse
hooves. The mix felt funny and right, all the obedient drudgery
expected of women and horses. I'd used a bunch of silver gelatin
prints of women's button-up leather work boots mixed with the
close-ups of the hooves. I mixed things up, too, with a few capsules filled with steel particles I'd swept together from the floor.
The diagonal had needed something else that didn't bring hu-
mans to mind, some element that would outlive us all. I'd added

a rock with the shine of some mica in it. Also a curl of the parchment-like bark from the one birch tree out back that hadn't died yet.

One week, I got into acorns, gluing them like heads onto the sawed-off bottom half of plastic soldier figurines from the flea market, and why not? What else made the soul ring as loudly as remaking the shape of something that doesn't want to give, having a tool in your hand powerful enough to melt some ugly piece of junk metal down so fast you could see it happen, the little puddle of silver liquid where there had been solid metal a minute before? It mesmerized me every time, how fast I could turn four pieces of scrap metal into a shape, create that darkness that forms inside a box. Like Agnes repeating her calming grids, the obscurity inherent in a lidded box just kept calling me.

I'd love to scale way up, if you're willing to help, I told Elliott. The thought of getting to weld beyond the weight and size of what I could maneuver on my own was so thrilling it caused a fresh throb of pain in my leg. I lurched out of the chair to see if moving might help, but the throb only got worse.

Shit, I said, tipping enough on the crutches that Elliott had to grab hold of my arm to keep me upright.

I better stop for today and lie down, I told him, but you're welcome to stay and use the shower. It's really no problem, if you'd like, after all the work you put in.

I reached into my pocket for the three twenties I'd placed there to pay him and asked if that was enough. He took the bills and nodded, lowering his face to his shoulder to wipe the sweat from his forehead on his filthy T-shirt.

Go on, I told him, you might as well. Nobody else using that shower.

He didn't hesitate for more than a second this time, before heading down the hall and into the bathroom, and I sensed how easily this could go on and sensed, too, my own arousal at the prospect. *All that seems like fantastic mistakes are not mistakes . . . it all has to be done*, Agnes promised, though she was talking about errors on a canvas, not errors with others.

Whatever the case, once I sank into the cushions in the den, I let my mind do as it pleased at the clink of the metal shower rings in the bathroom. At the first splash of water, I imagined Elliott facing away from the showerhead, the water warming as it ran over his broad, pimpled face and bony shoulders.

I'd thought I was beyond feeling any desire for a man anywhere near me, and yet here I was, electrified at the possibility of Elliott in there, pissing in the shower as Dave used to do, of Elliott's toes no longer sealed in his boots, his urine streaming between his feet, the yellow of it fading with the water as it vanished down the drain.

At the thought of Elliott's cock, my chest tightened, my heart ticking faster under my ribs, and I let go of my thigh, the awful clamor of the pain there. I tuned myself to the sounds in the bathroom instead and it felt like tuning in to life itself—the creak of the towel rack. The thump of Elliott's damp, bare foot on the floor. I saw the crack in his skinny behind, the trickles of water coursing down his legs, the dampness of his feet on my gray bath mat. I pictured his arm reaching for one of my blue hand towels, rubbing himself dry between his legs, and I felt the disobedience that still flowed in me, the potency of it. Such a welcome jolt, I felt it all over—and what did it matter what thought brought on the surge of that energy, if it was a few randy thoughts about a young man who could snap my neck if he felt like it?

Elliott could dump me on the floor like a broken lamp and what would come of it? Nothing. He could make that choice anytime, though he hadn't yet.

LEAH

We are passing such bleak, derelict houses on this block. I want Jean's house to stand out somehow. I can't picture her living under a roof with so many blistered, curled-up shingles and tar patches. She worked long enough at the hospital to have Social Security, I would imagine, enough savings at least to maintain a decent roof on her parents' house and keep a little vitality going. Surely there will be something distinctively Jean on the porch that I will recognize, one of her weird finds from the flea market, like the dented pig-shaped weathervane she brought home once, which caused a prolonged argument with my father, who found the weathervane tacky and refused to let Jean plant her tin pig anywhere, even half hidden among the bushes in the backyard. Living solely on her own terms now, surely she would have something funny in her yard or on the porch, maybe even one of her towers, some bright paint on the front door.

In case I'm conjuring yet another errant fairy tale for my stepmother, I pay attention to the numbers on the houses, too. Or I do to the houses that still have numbers rusting on the mailbox or on the porch pillars. We've arrived in early September at five p.m., the day still warm and bright, the grass dotted with dandelions and other vaguely familiar weedy blooming things that Jean used to name in the car with me. She liked shouting out the names that made her laugh. Check out those shithouse beauties, she would say. Here comes some good-lookin' joe, see that pye weed there?

I have no recall of what names might belong to the blooming weeds we are passing now, or whether, on those terrifying visits to see Jean's father, we pulled into a house in the middle of this block or on the corner, how its shape differed from the similar two-story homes and single-car driveways before and after it.

That must be Elliott, Gerardo says, pointing at a scrawny man hunched over on the front steps of a house to the right of us, with a porch as irrevocably collapsing as all the others. There is no bright door. No gingerbread roof. Jean has resorted to the same splotches of tar as everyone else. Now that we've reached the house, I recognize the bushes along the side and the garage on the left, the four concrete squares leading from the driveway.

On the front steps, Elliott lifts his head and the shock hits me with physical force. I press my whole body backward against the seat as Gerardo brings our rental car to a stop in the driveway.

Don't get out, I tell him.

Why? He looks fine, he's just sitting there, Gerardo says, turning the engine off.

No, he's not fine, I say. He was one of them, in the woods.

The fear I felt that night with Jean in the forest comes back to me so fast I get light-headed. I explain to Gerardo that Elliott was one of the drunk men who showed up on the cliff, the one who'd known Jean.

I try to keep my face neutral, aware of Elliott watching us through the windshield.

Are you sure? Gerardo asks and I admit that I'm not sure. So much about Elliott's clothing and appearance adheres to the visual code of all the young men here. His buzzed head and unlaced construction boots. His baggy jeans and the unnerving blankness of his expression.

On the phone, when Elliott called, I assumed he was in his fifties or sixties, a man close to Jean's age. He didn't say anything about our having met each other once. He told me nothing beyond his intended reason for the call, which I assumed was connected to his unease relaying his version of Jean's death and explaining the immensity of the numerous towers she'd assembled in the house, his need for me to come here and do something about them. He seemed sober and coherent on that call, his curt replies nothing like the slurred drunk voice from that night in the woods. In every news clip of young men with buzzed heads and bulletproof vests, that slurred voice from my last trip has come back to me, his whole crew laughing in chilling unison on the cliff.

For a moment, the only movement anywhere between where I remain, sealed in the rental car with my family, and where Elliott remains, seated on the porch step, is the slight breeze moving the long blades of grass in the yard and the clumps of grass poking up through the broken planks of the steps.

We should get out, Leah, Gerardo says. We could just stand outside with him and see how it goes. It'll only get more awkward if we keep sitting here in the car like this. Let's at least get out and talk to him.

Already it feels charged, how long we have hesitated, staring out at Elliott through the windshield. We've come all this way and it's entirely possible I'm mistaken. I know I should reach for the door handle instead of clutching the sides of the cardboard pastry box on my lap. Except I don't want to give this box of goodwill gobs and peanut butter buckeyes to Elliott. I don't want to go anywhere near him. I'm certain now I know his pale, pitted face from that night in the woods. From the way he's staring at me through the windshield, I'm certain that he recognizes me as well.

JEAN

Elliott showed up on time every morning that first week working together. On Friday, before his sister made her usual exit for school and his mom for the deli, a run-down blue van pulled into their driveway. I'd yet to hear anyone pull in next door. A few times in the evening, I'd seen a compact red Honda stop at the curb for his sister. She'd come running out and join the group of girls crammed inside.

To hear a rattling van pull into their driveway this early in the morning was a surprise. It wasn't even eight yet. On the power line out front, the birds were still conducting their morning discussions, the clouds still low over the valley.

The van that pulled in looked like it might not make it back out. The entire bottom edge was corroded and someone had taped strips of West Virginia chrome over the worst of the rust. Duct tape may be what people call that solution elsewhere, though how people elsewhere would categorize what was holding a minivan together in Sevlick felt less relevant every year.

Through my front window, I watched Elliott and his mother stop together at the edge of the driveway. I saw his mother wave at the woman in the driver's seat, who had a similar attractive smile and darker skin tone than Elliott's sister, who was the only one moving toward the van. From the bereft look on his mother's slack face, it was clear something major was going on. When the sister slid the rusted side door of the van open, the mother gave one little limp wave and immediately crossed her arms again like they were all that was keeping her erect.

Beside his mother, Elliott kept his hands plunged in his pockets and didn't help his sister yank her two overfilled garbage bags into the van, both of them stuffed to the point of bursting. One of the kids inside the van started to help her lift the bags, sending a plastic hairbrush tumbling toward the driveway. The sister grabbed for her hairbrush with a fired-up quickness that felt familiar. I'd moved as fast as I could when I first left this street, too.

Watching her frenzied determination not to lose that brush or anything else in her bags, I half forgot about Elliott until the van rattled off and I saw he was still hunkering beside his mother, maintaining his usual mask of opacity, his reddening cheeks the lone indication that watching his sister flee with this other family might be catalyzing something unmanageable inside him.

He knocked on my door about an hour later. He'd begun coming over earlier, closer to nine, when it was cooler and we could get the harder work done before the heat rose, or Elliott got the work done, as I was still fairly useless. The soreness in my leg around the incision had lessened after a week, and I could handle the TIG torch sitting down now, so long as Elliott lifted the metal sheets and adjusted everything on the workbench while I sat there, doing nothing but the pedal and the weld. And

I made sure to let him get some welding in as well, guiding his hand with my own, showing him exactly how close to hold the torch for the sheet metal to turn molten and puddle up. I couldn't help bracing for him to get defensive at my corrections, to say something contemptuous as my father would have done, and as Dave had done relentlessly, and Dennis, my boss in the billing department, whose mind could proceed in only one direction at a time, like a lawn mower.

Still, I couldn't shake my mistrust of Elliott's humility. Or his willingness to hear me out on everything I'd learned from You-Tube. Something in me couldn't stop waiting for him to try to even the scales, to go after me with some insult about being too old or too odd or to simply call me a bitch.

If his humility was only a performance, he was remarkably good at it. He listened so intently I got him tack-welding with pretty good accuracy in two days. He learned much faster than I had, with no actual live human in the room to point out what I was getting wrong and what adjustment would correct it.

In less than a week, the beauty of those hours became manifest in a totem-shaped Manglement that took my breath away. With Elliott's help, the Manglement rose six feet high with its cockeyed lid on. I asked him to carry in my father's ladder from the garage. I'd known I could go higher if I brought that ladder inside, but it was far too heavy for me to move on my own. Once Elliott set up the ladder, welding the totem went so fast it felt like we'd worked our way to heaven and back.

In the evening, after a can of Progresso soup, I limped in circles around that glorious, enormous totem like I was the ticking hand of a clock. It was the closest I'd known to contentment in years, watching the lowering sunlight refract off the camera lenses on the front of the capsules, their delightful spiral up the four metal sides. *A contentment with oneself*, Agnes wrote, *that is success.* With the sides of the totem nearly reaching the ceiling, the spiral of photos in the capsules really came alive. To see all those photos I'd collected of women's dingy boots, magnified in their capsules and twisting up six feet of sheet metal, felt like a resurrection.

That morning the van arrived, I'd entered the living room feeling so triumphant even the clumsy portrait of Leah on the wall had failed to cause its usual sting of remorse. All I could think about was Elliott coming through the door and getting started. Until that morning his sister left, he'd seemed more content as well, letting out a soft whistle of satisfaction each time he'd gotten a tack weld just right.

Once that van arrived for his sister, though, something shifted. Elliott entered the house an hour later sullen and surly, an unnerving tightness to his movements. He said nothing as he came in, just clomped in his unlaced boots into the front room and headed straight to the kitchen like this was his own house. I hobbled after him, asking if everything was all right.

All right? Nothing's been all right for a long fuckin' time, Elliott said, pouring himself a glass of water from the sink.

I asked who'd come in the van. After he gulped down the whole glass, he explained about Paulina, his sister's aunt on her father's side. It was the first I'd heard about Elliott being raised by a stepfather named Manuel, who'd died two years ago of stomach cancer.

When I asked if he'd liked Manuel, Elliott slammed his glass down with an abruptness I didn't expect.

I fuckin' loved him. Everyone loved Manuel, he said and I told him I was sorry. Agitated, his face red and twitchy, he explained about the medical debt that had led to the loss of their house over in Elkdale, how absolutely nothing had gone right since then.

I'm sure Jackie will stay with Paulina and them for good, he said. I would if they were my family. My mom gits it, though, he said. And she knows I'm not gonna leave her.

She's lucky to have you, I said.

Like hell she is.

He gripped the counter on either side of him. It was payin' off my crap, he said, that fucked us over. And with my record, I can't get hired for shit.

He kicked his heel back against the cabinet beneath the sink before stepping away and I didn't ask any more. I kept my distance as he clomped wordlessly ahead of me back toward the front room and flipped on the argon gas without asking. I didn't think he was in a calm enough state to start welding. I didn't stop him, though, when he slipped the helmet down over his head and pulled my leather gloves over his hands.

So. What do you want me to do for you? he asked. You want another box?

I didn't like the contempt in his tone at all, the hostility in the way he'd spit out the word *box*, although I understood it. Every day coming down the stairs I had to get through all kinds of contempt for my endless boxes, their hold on me. A disdain for my own aspirations rose up my throat like acid reflux at the sight of all the mangled-up boxes I couldn't stop making. For daring to wake up thinking about Art, to think it needed me. To think what I was doing in here was anything more than indulgent, delusional foolishness. Who needed my pitiful attempt on Paton Street at some new kind of beauty?

No one.

And yet every particle in my body longed to make six more sides, rivet them together.

Yep, I told Elliott, a box is the plan for today. And for tomorrow. I'd like your help with a horizontal Manglement. You know, about casket-size. That all right with you?

He let out a nervous laugh and said that was fine.

I didn't dare brush up against any part of Elliott that morning his sister took off. Once he got focused, he seemed calmer, and I explained the new Manglement, the long shape of it that would rest along the floor instead of rising like a totem, its heavy sides dented with a hammer.

Like someone trying to bang their way out, he said. I like that.

Exactly, I said. That's exactly what I had in mind.

I nodded at him, not expecting my eyes to fill, just describing out loud this idea I'd been holding on to since Leah was a child, and to hear Elliott say *I like that.*

I listened with all my being to his movements in the bathroom that day Jackie left. I imagined the water trickling down the crook of his skinny neck, over his bony chest and nipples.

Elliott didn't emerge from the bathroom that Friday in his usual ten minutes. He stayed under the water so long it felt like a question, as if he, too, wanted to push things and see what might happen. The water ran and ran in the shower, my body aching in a way I'd thought would be gone by my age.

Finally I got up, swung on my crutches out of the den, thumping on down the hall until I was just outside the bathroom. Once my back was against the wall, I felt immediately more alive, hearing every rustle on the other side of the door, the elastic snap of what had to be the band of Elliott's underwear.

He emerged from the bathroom too abruptly for me to slide down the wall. At the sight of me just outside the door, he squinted and tilted his head to one side the way one might upon noticing a sudden hissing sound coming from somewhere within the house. For a moment, our faces were so close in the dark hall, I could have licked the scar on his lip if I'd bent my head in his direction.

I waited to see what Elliott would do. He didn't lean closer. He didn't step back. He just stood there like he was locked in place.

Guess I'll, uhh . . . see you tomorrow, he said.

I guess so, I replied and stepped back for him to make his way out of the house, and he did.

Once I heard the door creak shut, I swung on my crutches into the bathroom and pressed my face to the damp hand towels. I felt wolfish breathing in the faint sweaty smell he'd left on them. I went on breathing in the trace of him, relishing it with my whole face.

When I'd read "Little Red Riding Hood" to Leah at bedtime, she liked for me to read the wolf's lines in an exaggeratedly wicked voice, to allow for no confusion about whether I was speaking as the wolf or the grandma. For a school-age child, it felt fine, eliminating the confusion at the heart of things that way. Although wasn't the truth otherwise—couldn't a person be well intentioned most of the time, and for just a few minutes each afternoon become the ravenous wolf?

I liked teaching Elliott, making him sandwiches. I wasn't just after the trace of him on my hand towels. At the thought of him arriving tomorrow morning, what he might think if I put out a full-size towel for him, I got agitated. I ate through an entire bag of caramel creams on the couch, flipping for the millionth time through the photos of Louise's sculptures of peripheral people awaiting their turn. My favorite was the bare pole she'd chosen to depict the restless life of a woman named Catherine Yarrow, a bare pole and a cluster of rusty nails, all of them hammered at the level of the human heart.

In the afternoon, I heard Elliott at the spigot, filling the first of their gallon jugs. He stopped after his customary four and shut off the spigot, and it seemed entirely possible we could just continue as we had.

The next morning, I got prepped and ready for his arrival, ran my palms over the metal sheets where he'd left them on the floor, imagining the Manglement they would become, the shape I'd been walking around in my mind now for over two decades. The idea had come to me driving away from this house once with Leah. I remembered the exact afternoon, passing the same two-story, ordinary houses I'd been passing my entire life when I saw it in my mind, the great dented casket I would weld someday to seal shut over my father's voice. The idea had struck me as funny until I couldn't stop imagining his muffled threats coming from under a casket lid I'd welded with his own drill bit. The juicy satisfaction of the idea became like a magical stick of gum that never lost its flavor. I started to picture the dents in the metal sides, the poke of my father's sharp elbows, the kick of his heels— the futile dents of his furious resistance and the lid sealed.

Very special power tools, the Great Louise called them, all the noisy options that would not have been possible in another century. She'd used all kinds of machines in her *Destruction of the Father*, had devised a whole plaster meal of her dad, serving him up in little sly mounds like a tray of whoopie pies. I'd been ready to serve up my own father for some time now, and how filling it would be, to feast my eyes each morning on that long heavy box for him at last, to weld it shut with my own hands.

I checked the clock to see how soon Elliott would come, if he was coming. It had been a terrible, stupid impulse to go creeping up like that, right outside the bathroom. Before this morning, he'd been arriving no later than 9:30, and it was already 10:03. The front room was getting humid, filling with summer heat.

If he didn't show up soon, I guessed I could try going over and floating some sort of explanation. I could tell him it was just bad timing, that I'd been heading to the kitchen on my crutches and lost my balance, had to lean against the wall just as he was opening the bathroom door. Even if he didn't believe me, I could try to lure him back, make it clear that the boundary would be set now. We could just pretend yesterday hadn't happened.

At 10:10, I swung on my crutches around the two workbenches, pulled out the ball-peen hammer I hoped would allow
Elliott to make the sharp dents as I'd pictured them. Yesterday
we'd suspended the sheet metal, supporting it a few inches off
the floor with some other bits of scrap. With the sheet metal
suspended off the floor that way, I hoped Elliott could make the
dents with the ball-peen alone. What I really needed to get the
dents right was an oxyacetylene torch. I'd never even looked for
one at the fleas or yard sales, never imagining I might actually
come to make this Manglement in tandem with another person
who could do the hitting while I operated the heat.

I peered out the window, checked my watch, imagined Elliott
sitting in his house right now, doing nothing but staying away
from me. At a quarter after, I couldn't take it. I started on my
crutches toward the front door, intending to peer out just enough
to see if he was outside, slumped on his front steps as if he'd never
entered my house. Maybe we were about to start a tense new era
of living beside each other, pretending we were strangers.

When I opened the door, I found him on my front lawn, about
to come up the steps.

Hey, how ya doin', Hounslow? You ready to get goin'? I asked
in my brassiest voice.

Elliott yanked his head up in surprise and I didn't mention
the time, the lateness of his arrival. I just kept talking at him,
upping my enthusiasm to keep things jangling, hoping to just
move forward and never have to talk about yesterday. Hunched
over in his bull's-eye shirt, he pressed his hands into his jeans

pockets and clomped up the steps. I saw he had a new pimple on his broad pale forehead.

I hope you're feeling ready to hammer the shit out of that sheet, I said, reiterating my longing for an oxyacetylene torch, how I wished he wasn't helping an artist so lacking in resources. I pulled out the ball-peen I thought would give the best shape for the dents.

You really got the idea yesterday, Hounslow, I said, of someone trapped in there, with the dents giving the idea of angry heels and someone throwing a real fit under the lid.

I'll try, Elliott mumbled with an edge to his voice that made me feel wretched, a decrepit old queen barking orders at a servant.

His first few blows didn't leave even the slightest dent and I heard him swear under his breath. He didn't look at me and I didn't ask him to keep trying, though he did, the veins standing out from the effort in his stringy arms. When he hit harder, the metal sheet started to warp, even when I moved the supports closer. I told him to stop for a minute. I didn't want him to warp the metal any more than he already had, and the dents he'd made were barely noticeable, not anything like the poke of sharp elbows and knees I'd imagined, none of the energy and movement I'd been picturing while I sat in my cubicle in the hospital, pretending that I was a reasonable, resigned woman, that I wasn't burning up inside trying to contain the desire to release what Agnes called one's most certain devotion.

After a few more futile blows, Elliott set the hammer down and shook the tension out of his hand, flicking his fingers back and forth, and I told him there was no need to keep trying. What I'd had in mind with the hammer was just wishful thinking, impossible without an oxyacetylene torch, which would run me five hundred bucks at least, to get both the oxygen and acetylene tanks and the torch. To even try with a hammer doesn't make sense, I admitted.

Well, doesn't make much sense to run a welder in the living room neither, Elliott said, and you already welded all them. He motioned toward the back wall, the shelves that had once been filled with my mother's painted plate collection, now crammed with all the lopsided Manglements I'd already managed in here on my own. To bask in the glow of his noticing for a moment felt wonderful. Just to stand there, enjoying his acknowledgment of all I'd made, felt as bright as standing under moonlight.

I was just about to thank him when a loud rumbling escaped his stomach and his broad cheeks reddened. I didn't comment on the sound, just swung up onto my crutches and asked if I could fix him a bowl of cereal or some eggs.

I'm all right, he said, his stomach defying him and emitting an even louder rumble. I felt awful, monstrous to have just asked for reassurance for my futile attempts at Art while this young man was standing there ravenous. My God.

Come on, I told him, crutching ahead to the kitchen before he could object again. I wanted to ask what he'd done with the $150 in cash I'd paid him last week. I hoped the reason he hadn't used it for groceries was because he and his mother had paid whatever they owed to restore their water service instead. The monthly rate for my house was sixty dollars. I hoped what I was paying

Elliott each week would be more than enough to restore their water and avoid eviction.

I didn't bring any of this up, not wanting him to think I was out to judge him. I just got him a cereal bowl and my box of cinnamon oat squares. While he slurped at his first bowl, I set up my laptop on the table and we clicked through the most-watched videos for making dents with an acetylene torch, watching the sheet metal in the videos heating up instantly to a searing orange, nearly blue, malleable enough to dent exactly as I'd imagined. Twice we watched a video of a wild-eyed man who kept making a strange hooting sound every time he brought down his sledgehammer.

I sure as hell wouldn't want to work for him, Elliott said, getting up to take his cereal bowl to the sink. He seemed far more relaxed now that he'd eaten and I decided his agitation when he arrived was just hunger and not about where he'd found me yesterday, lurking outside the bathroom door.

I was about to ask if he was ready to get back to work when he turned around, dug his hands into the baggy pockets of the filthy carpenter jeans he wore every day, and told me they'd gotten the notice yesterday. I asked if he meant from the city, avoiding the word *eviction* as he had, aware of the uneasy energy of his body pushing back against my sink.

But you have cash now, right, from what I've paid you so far?

Not for the fuckin' penalty, he said. Paying the deposit isn't enough for those fuckers. He turned his face toward the fridge and explained about the three-hundred-dollar deposit the city demanded if a family didn't have an account in good standing, the merciless eighty-dollar penalty for reinstallation on top of that.

They won't give nobody back their water, he said, without leaving you fuckin' broke. The veins stood out in his arms and along his neck as he stated this, his cheeks flushing redder than usual.

What a bunch of bastards, I said, nervous about what to offer and what Elliott might expect next from me if I did. To give him the entire amount they needed to avoid eviction could backfire all sorts of ways, with him asking for more, and then the need to say yes again, or to say no the next time and burden our hours together, blowing a new problem into the room that would leave us both unable to talk with any ease, or speak on instinct about the next tower, which would probably turn out awkward, too.

It felt cruel, though, and conniving for the decision to be about Elliott continuing to help with the Manglements, about my small attempts at Art. He needed the cash to keep his family from getting evicted.

I lowered my head, breathing in the silent leak of his desperation, filling the kitchen like argon gas, giving off no hiss or smell, only a fatal heaviness to the air. I picked at the scab on my thumb from a cut I'd done with an X-Acto blade over a month ago. The skin on my hands was so thin and slow to heal now, quick to bruise. My whole bodily operation had become miserably unreliable.

What I needed was a quiet minute to think about how to get this right.

How about you go and shower, I said slowly. That was a lot of hammering, I told him, and I can think a little about what I might be able to do to help.

I stayed in the kitchen while Elliott undressed in the bathroom. He seemed to take longer than usual to turn the water on. I listened same as I had each day, only now there was this answer pending and I didn't like it. I'd have to give him the money and help his family keep their house. I'd have to drive over to the bank after lunch and then make it clear I couldn't help with a large amount again, only this once.

It felt quieter than ever in the house then, sitting in the kitchen alone, waiting for Elliott to finish up in the shower. The splashing sound on the other side of the bathroom door was so ordinary yet unbearable, the water I had and he didn't, that difference that was always there.

No other louder sound outside overtook the muffled flow of water, no howl from Steve's sad, trapped hound, no truck revving past, and after a few minutes, my mind went ahead and did what it had each day, picturing what Elliott might be up to next with my soap. Except it felt gross to me this time. I tried to flush the pleasure out of my mind like it was a toilet. To be a decent person, I just needed to push the handle down and clean my thoughts.

Knock it off, you sick son of a bitch, I murmured to myself. And yet my imagination wouldn't obey. I imagined the jut of his hip bones, his cock going soft under the hot water, his dark pubic hair.

I didn't expect the bathroom door to open so soon after the water stopped. I thought my revved-up mind was to blame when Elliott stepped into the kitchen with only his jeans on and his chest bare. I thought I was losing all sense of reality, seeing him without a shirt on, his sharp hips protruding just as I'd pictured them. The faint line of his ribs was just as I'd pictured it, too, visible through the paler skin usually hidden under his shirt. It was the raised keloid scar across his chest that set off my recognition. I wasn't imagining Elliott under his clothes. There was his actual chest in the doorway, a scar thick as an inchworm across the indent between his ribs. His body looked so close to malnourished my heart clamped.

Elliott, what in the world, I said.

It's okay, he said in a tense voice that was a good distance from okay. His expression was plaintive, fearful even, not at all how I'd pictured his reaction when I'd imagined pulling back the plastic curtain liner on the shower. Nothing was right about the reluctant, anguished way he moved from the doorway into the kitchen, his bare chest bony and hairless as a boy's. He stepped right up to the wooden chair where I was sitting, wedging his knees between my own.

Elliott, what's going on here? I asked him.

Oh c'mon, you were just out in the hall yesterday, he said, you were listening to me dry off with those little fuckin' towels.

But I didn't mean for you—

What did you mean then, asking me to go shower? he asked.

Not this, I murmured, shaking my head.

Although what had I meant? I didn't quite know. I couldn't think of any answer that would be adequate with Elliott remaining where he'd come to a stop in front of me, our knees touching, my face right up against the pale knot of his belly button. I stared at all the tight, tight folds of skin inside it.

I didn't move when he grabbed one of my tits, loose under my shirt. All of it felt rotten, irrefutably ruinous. Like the floor of the kitchen had just given way and we'd sunk together into some crumbling realm full of termites. I felt the silent crawling of them all over my skin.

I'd never thought of myself as a person who made anything happen, who had any power over anyone. I couldn't grasp how I'd done it, Elliott thinking I was asking for this if he didn't want it, grabbing my tit even if it required this dread-filled look on his face. When had I ceased to be harmless? Had I ever been?

I can do it, he said, it's okay.

He didn't let up the pressure of his grip on my tit and I didn't move, though the chair felt ruthlessly hard against my back, the quiet around us even harder, with no give at all, no mercy—and I had none for myself.

This isn't right, Elliott, honestly, you misunderstood, I told him, tensing for his reaction, for him to hit me with the force of his humiliation.

I'll help your family as much as I can but not like this, I added, careful to keep my head down, my gaze on his chest, that awful raised pink scar as he dug his thumb deeper into the loose skin of my tit until it hurt.

Still, I didn't move. I just kept my head down, waiting for him to clobber me.

Please stop, I whispered. Go put your shirt on, Elliott, please.

The words scratched my throat, harsh and sharp as metal dust. He let out a sound of disbelief, or maybe it was disgust. Whatever that sound was about, Elliott shut down after it. He didn't let another sound escape his mouth, didn't allow himself the release of even a single word. He just backed away, bare, bony-chested, and silent as he'd come in.

I didn't dare raise my head or call to him when he left the house. I stayed exactly where I was, listening to the familiar shuffle of his heavy, unlaced boots cutting a path through my Manglements, and then the slap of the screen door. It occurred to me that the best course of action to help his family would be to wait until that evening or, better yet, walk over with a check in the morning, a generous four hundred bucks to help get their water restored and restore my sense of decency in the process.

I felt far from decent, though, lying awake in my bed half the night. It had seemed so minor, leaving Elliott in there making do without a towel each day, pretending there was nothing odd going on.

And why had I let it get odd and odder? I could have made him feel taken care of in the bathroom here, given him a bottle of shampoo and a new bar of soap along with a folded towel of his own. I could have done that for him, treated him more like a grown child, which he was—he was younger than Leah. Except there'd been all that male energy of his, that unbidden strength in his arms, that possibility of killing me anytime.

In the morning, I got nervous about going over, seeing Elliott in his own doorway. I decided to wait until ten or so, when they were definitely all awake and I could just leave the check on the porch, knock on the door, and leave. Once he got his family's water reconnected, maybe he would come and knock at my door again. He'd have no need to shower here anymore and we could start over, on a new tower. He'd be a good-enough welder soon to take on other side jobs, if he wanted, for extra money.

Yet before ten a.m. came around, something else happened

instead. The same rusted van rattled up and pulled in, with its sad strip of West Virginia chrome along the rusted bottom of the sliding door. The same kind-faced aunt was at the wheel, Jackie looking small in the passenger seat beside the aunt, peering out from behind her loose hair with a pained, nervous face.

I kept back from the window to watch them. The first to step out of the van was a teenage boy with shaggy dark hair that reached his shoulders. He helped Elliott carry two misshapen, worn-looking mattresses out of the house and secure them to the roof of the van with a striped rope.

I hadn't thought whether Elliott and his family might have been short a mattress at night, having to share two between the three of them. The meager number of cardboard boxes that emerged from their house made my heart ache. Elliott made his way around the van, knotting the striped rope over the two mattresses, the teenage boy shadowing his movements around the van, giving the striped rope an extra pull as soon as Elliott let go. I waited for him to look over at my house, dreading what sort of expression might come over his face.

He didn't look over once, or not that I saw. Only his mother did, her mouth turned down in what I took to be disgust. Or her look was just dread—maybe she knew nothing of what had gone on with her son in my house. My mind went blank at the shame of it. I had the check ready. I could step outside now and offer it to them, just hand it to Elliott without a word and go back inside.

No, if I was going to go out there, I'd have to apologize. At least look him in the eye and not be a coward.

Or I could be a coward and do nothing. Just be an absolute wolf and keep on hiding where I was, out of their sight line, watching them through the front window. I'd never have to provide an honest answer to anyone about what had gone on. Who would ever ask?

I felt grateful for my isolation then, for how used to isolation we all were on this street and in these old-as-coal mountains. I wouldn't be obliged to have any kind of reckoning with anyone about what had gone on with Elliott in my house. I could stick him down in the sod of my mind and continue with my days as if he'd never come through the door. Except he had, and I could feel it now, the sharp dent of him in my chest. The hole already there where Leah had been. Oh, what a relief it was to know there would be nobody seeing my face today. Wasn't that the upside of retreating from the world? No pressure to explain things out loud, to make any sense to other people, or even much sense to yourself.

After one last tug on the striped rope securing his family's two mattresses, Elliott ducked his head and slipped into the van. The aunt started up her rattling engine and I knew that was the last I'd see of him.

LEAH

W hy aren't we getting out? Is this the place? Silvestre asks from the back seat and I assure him this is it— the place we meant to reach.

Except I never meant to reach this place, to be in proximity with Elliott again. Jean knew how repellent I found him and his friends, how frantic I was to get away from them. I can't picture her intending to trick me into coming back here to see her towers just to trap me in a situation with Elliott once again. Jean wasn't conniving in that way and hadn't lived with mortality at the front of her mind.

Although she must have thought about dying at some point, enough to draw up a will.

In all my fairy tale conjuring, I didn't account for the possibility that I'd be the one who'd fail to anticipate the twist. Unbuckling Silvestre, I hear Jean's laughter again that night in the woods, her shouts in the truck defending Elliott and his friends like her very existence depended on her allegiance to them. The memory is so destabilizing it takes me four tries to extract Silvestre from his car seat, my fingers too clumsy with shock to hit the center of the buttons in order to unlock the straps.

At the gas station, I had such a strong feeling that we should turn around. I'd recognized how naive we were being about Elliott, that I had no grasp from one phone call of who he was, the likelihood that he was as racist and unhinged as the woman at the next pump. Maybe I've never really had any grasp on who Jean was either.

My last trip here I made the same mistake, jumping into Jean's truck, as trusting and eager for her attention as if I were still ten years old. That trip I came alone with my father. The one friend he'd kept from our years in Sevlick had died, a librarian he had liked at the county hospital where he'd also met Jean. I was newly back to the U.S., relishing our nascent life in New York, where I assumed I'd be able to get a connecting flight to the tiny airport in Sevlick I remembered, with a single runway.

That nothing airport? Oh, that's long gone, my father told me on the phone. It closed over a decade ago. He said there was no operating runway in any of the Allegheny Mountain towns around Sevlick either. The surrounding towns had become equally unreachable, isolated as an archipelago, the only airports a considerable distance away, in Pittsburgh or Cleveland.

I balked at the six-hour drive, but my father reminded me that I'd been living on another continent for over a decade. We hadn't taken a trip together since I was in college, and after all my years living in another language, I felt ready to see Jean again, show off my fully formed adult self to her. I was proud of the first job I'd found at a bilingual children's press, and of Gerardo, who'd been hired as an interpreter at a news service. We'd joined an

international film club full of fascinating people and I didn't
pause or panic before taking a seat at the table.

Four years ago, when I emailed Jean about the trip with my
father, she answered right away. We made a vague plan for her to
pick me up outside Sevlick's lone hotel, a run-down Holiday Inn
where my father had booked a room, and where I've booked a
room again for tonight, with my family. I didn't tell my father
about my plans to see Jean until my long drive with him was
nearly over. I knew the immediate tension the plan would cause.

What do you need to see her for? he asked.

Because she was good to me, I told him.

I hope she brings you back alive, he said. Who knows what
she's been doing since the hospital closed. I don't know if you
realize how far down the tubes this area has gone.

It'll be fine, I assured him, and Jean arrived right on time in
the parking lot of the Holiday Inn. Her giant blue pickup truck
was a surprise and yet also Jean-like in its roaring enormity. I felt
a glow under my skin at the sight of her behind the windshield,
waving at me. As soon as I climbed in, she grabbed my hands, her
voice as loud and emphatic as I remembered, the immediate heat
of her company like stepping into the onrush of a wildfire.

You've got the same earnest face, Leah, the very same, she told
me, squeezing my palms with alarming force, and I was startled
at how good it felt, the familiar intensity of her grip. I knew
you'd keep that earnest face, she declared. A hundred women
your age, she told me, could have stepped out of that hotel and I
would've recognized you in an instant. You know that, right?

I told her of course and didn't dare retract my hands from her grasp. Her gray hair was a shock. None of her hair was the reddish brown that I remembered. She'd kept her hair just as long, though, and still pulled back with the same thick red rubber bands from the kitchen that she'd used on my hair twenty years before, insisting they didn't hurt as much as I complained they did. I'd forgotten the small, raised mole below her eye, but there it still was, on the looser, thinned skin of her face. Her wide smile revealed the same chip on her right front tooth, and the dark scrutiny in her brown eyes hadn't changed either.

I would have recognized you in an instant, too, I lied, and saw the immediate pleasure on Jean's face. The reliable rewards of pleasing her came right back to me as we pulled out of the parking lot of the Holiday Inn. I'd thought it was from my father that I'd learned to anticipate what others wanted to hear. I'd forgotten how intently I'd honed that skill early with Jean, too.

She suggested that we catch the sunset up on Burton Rock. What do you think? she asked. I'm feeling nostalgic, she explained, with you so grown up. She asked if I remembered our picnic dinners together on that ledge when my dad was working late, making up songs together on the path through the woods.

Of course I remember, I told her, and to prove it, I asked if she still made the ham, butter, and lettuce sandwiches we'd brought to eat on the cliff, and she let out a whistling sound, reaching over for my hand once again.

I knew you didn't forget me. I just knew it, Jean said, blowing me a kiss, and then she warned that we were cutting it close. The sun is gonna be shot in about ten minutes but I don't give a damn, do you?

I shrugged and said I was up for anything, and at that point, I was. It was so exhilarating to be with her again, relishing the familiar eagerness in her voice, determined to convince me of whatever she'd already decided we were going to do. She kept laughing in loud gulping bursts about my remembering those ham-and-butter sandwiches.

God how I've missed you, kid, you have no idea, she repeated as she sped on through a yellow light, explaining that we were going to have to walk fast to reach the cliff before the sun gave up, and the trail would likely be muddy. You used to be an expert puddle jumper, Jean said. Do you remember those little red rain boots I got for you, with the painted dots on the front like ladybugs?

Not wanting to disappoint her, I nodded, though I didn't remember the boots.

When we arrived, the path through the woods to the ledge was indeed full of puddles. Even the edges of the path were sodden with thick mud, making for a more slippery walk than I'd expected. I didn't comment on the number of empty beer cans, bottles, and random socks strewn along the path. I didn't remember walking past random discarded things on our treks through these woods, although I did remember being on a trail in the same woods with Jean when a man emerged with a shotgun and said we'd crossed onto his property. When I brought up that man, she laughed and said she'd forgotten about that asshole and hoped he was dead.

Let's talk about something better than that, she said. Tell me about this good-looking husband you found and about living all the way in South America. I bet that was wild, huh?

I told her about my enjoyable life in Lima, which had not been particularly wild at all. When we reached the flat rocks out to the cliff, I was surprised at how ghostly the town looked from above, with so many empty streets, such a vast ugly mess of abandoned lots and buildings where the steel mill had been along the river.

Absolutely gorgeous, right? Jean said. Everyone who leaves here forgets how incredible these mountains are until they come back. I bet you forgot how beautiful it is here, didn't you? I bet you did, right?

She laughed at her own insistence, as she always had, and I nodded, knowing she wasn't really waiting for me to say yes. There was no need. I just focused on trying to enjoy what she saw, on the lush abundance of trees extending on both sides of us, instead of the hulking emptiness of the mills below. A great swoop of birds passed over the low clouds. The birds were plunging for a second time when I heard a sound moving closer, what sounded like the roar of a vehicle.

Is that coming from the dirt path? I asked Jean. Are people allowed to drive on that trail?

Sounds to me like an ATV, she said. Let's hope they're headed somewhere else.

A minute later, a roofless camo-painted vehicle appeared and four young men clambered out, clutching beers and joking around.

How you ladies doin' tonight? the tallest one asked, already striding toward us in his construction boots. When the skinny, smallest one climbed out, I saw his attention immediately drawn to Jean, and a stricken look on Jean's face as she inquired in a forced upbeat tone how he'd been. He shrugged, and I saw his eyes were bloodshot, his stare vacant, his pale wide forehead pitted with acne.

Fuckin' homeless is how I've been, he said. How 'bout you? He lifted his can of Pabst Blue Ribbon to his mouth and I noticed the scar in his lower lip thickened as it continued down onto his chin. He shrugged again when Jean told him she was sorry to hear this. He didn't seem to have any interest in telling her anything else. I thought she would agree when I announced the mosquitoes were getting awful and we should probably get going.

I didn't feel betrayed then, when Jean first ignored me. Of course she needed to be polite to this troubled young man who knew her. I thought she was just being gracious to ensure our safe return through the woods to her truck. I assumed she was eager to leave, too. When the skinny one took a step closer to us, I expected him to address Jean again.

I remember hearin' about you, he said, lifting his face in my direction.

In my shock, I thought that I'd misheard. About me? I asked and stepped back, away from him, sliding on the wet soles of my sandals, which were still slippery from the muddy path.

I waited for Jean to intervene, to explain to him that he was mistaken. Or for her just to recognize the need for us to get out of there, to use the mosquitoes as our excuse. She had survived in this town for over sixty years. She wouldn't linger on a rocky ledge with a bunch of drunk young men at sunset.

And yet Jean acted as if the comment about me from the strung-out skinny one hadn't happened. She just kept asking him polite questions, as if we were all standing in a supermarket and not on a darkening cliff.

Is everything all right with your sister? Jean asked him and then how his mother was getting along. His face slack, he turned away from her and didn't answer. She kept going with her questions as if she hadn't picked up on his reluctance to talk with her, or she didn't want to read the cues and recognize what seemed obvious to me. He was clearly on drugs and had no interest in responding to some older nosy woman he barely knew.

Except a beat later, he lifted his head and gave a delayed answer, that he didn't really know how his sister was doing. I was told I have a problem, he said, and to stay off the property.

Which is why those fuckers shouldn't be able to get no property, the tallest in the crew said, and the others laughed at once in a way that produced a lurching in my insides, how in sync the duration of their laughter was. Whatever coded insult the tallest one intended, they'd known exactly what reaction was expected, and they had delivered it with eagerness. The one who'd spoken to Jean was the only one who seemed out of step, which I attributed to whatever substance had left his eyes glassy and bloodshot.

Beyond the cliff, the sun was no more than a sliver now between the mountains and the sky. Keeping my panic to myself had become an all-consuming effort. If we didn't leave for Jean's truck soon, we were going to be stuck in the complete dark with these men and their chilling synchronicity.

Jean, my dad is really going to worry if we don't get back soon, I told her in a sterner tone.

Oh please, your dad can wait for once, it won't kill him, she snapped back.

All four of the men on the cliff laughed at this, and Jean laughed with them, tossing her head back like a girl. I was so appalled and shocked I said nothing, just watched as one of them turned to spit into the trees.

You ladies want a beer? the tallest one asked.

You bet I'll have one, Jean said, drawing closer to him.

How about you? the tall one asked me and I shook my head.

Oh c'mon, Leah, Jean said.

I don't want it, I told her. I want to go.

Suit yourself, she said. At the click of the tab on her beer, my anger spilled inward, toward my own poor judgment. My father had been right when he said in the hotel that I was being naive, thinking I could climb into a truck with Jean after two decades and trust her as I had as a child.

Closer to the cliff, Jean was now sipping away at her beer, her back to me, as if she were intent on forgetting that I was there, waiting for her. She let out another overly eager laugh and I went rigid with such a painful sense of abandonment I thought I might fall over. She had yet to look back to see if I was okay. She was postponing any thought of me, same as she must have done when she abruptly packed up and moved out. Along both sides of my skull, I felt a growing sense of pressure, an awful pulsing behind my eyes.

The heavyset one, who'd been quiet until now, crossed his arms and started talking in a hoarse voice about how easy it would be to pick off a deer in the grassy clearing below the ledge.

Wish I'd brought my Glock, he said.

I wouldn't even need a Glock, the tall one interjected, his head tipped back to slurp the last drops from his can. Anyone down there don't belong, I'd get him in one shot.

Fuck, I'd be fine with a six-shooter, the heavyset one replied, his voice defensive now, loud with bravado. If I spotted some fucker with no business bein' down there, I wouldn't have to move my finger more'n once. He wouldn't even know what hit 'im.

End of that bullshit, right? the tall one said. I've fuckin' had it with Jamel. I'm done with his black ass telling me how to dig a ditch.

You'd never take out Jamel, Pringle. You're too pussy, the heavyset one said. I'd get it done, though. I'd take out his black ass real fast, he declared with a laugh and then made a sudden popping sound with his mouth.

I didn't realize I'd visibly stiffened until he gestured toward me with his beer, the white lettering on the PBR can looking ominous, insidious in the dimming light.

Somethin' wrong? he asked, jutting his chin in my direction. The tall one turned toward me then, too, his eyes pausing on my breasts, before lowering his gaze to the zipper of my jeans.

I crossed my arms and told them no, that I was fine. I longed to take a step back and pull out my phone, mark my location. My legs tensed with the instinct to run off, though I knew it wasn't an option, not this far from town, or without Jean, and not now that these two men had tacitly made it clear what might happen if I didn't keep my contempt for them in check. Beyond the ledge, the sun had finished its descent behind the mountains, the last light no more than a faint orange glow against the clouds.

My whole body rang with fear. I felt like a giant bell, clanging to get off that cliff and away from those four drunk men. I called to Jean once more, where she was still standing out on the farthest rocks, her back to me, her full attention still on the skinny one with the glassy stare. Her fixation on him was baffling, why she was so reluctant to leave him.

We're going, Leah, she told me. Just let me finish this can, all right? She didn't bother to fully turn toward me as she said this, just lifted her beer again to her mouth, and whatever yearning I'd had for her company, for her affection, drained completely then, watching her continue to laugh with some strung-out drug addict young enough to be her child. A tightness had begun to build in my head and I couldn't stay still any longer. I started toward Jean, on the ledge, until the skinny one turned around and stumbled toward me instead.

You know, he said, I did wonder about you. The way your mom talked, I thought maybe you'd died or somethin'. He emitted a limp, drunk laugh, and I felt an internal tipping, as if the very axis of my being had lost its alignment.

My mom? I repeated.

Jean jerked her head up and looked right at me, at last.

I'm done, I told her, and the sunset, Jean, it's over.

I'd say it's been over for a while, the heavyset one spoke up with an edge of warning. I was sure I heard that edge of menace in his voice.

We're going right now, Jean promised, though even then she lifted her can of PBR to her mouth, for one last sip. I felt sick watching her and decided my father was right—she belonged to these psychopaths and to this town more than she ever had to me. Something about the threat in their energy, their fury, and her father's fury, was at her very core. She would sip their beer until they killed her. Or killed us both.

In the gathering dark, she looked much smaller and frailer than she had in the truck, with her bony wrists poking out from the rolled-up sleeves of her shirt. With her gray ponytail and narrow shoulders, she looked out of place next to their young male bodies and broader frames, the wide-stance sameness of their postures. Yet she kept laughing like she was one of them, throwing her head back to tip the remaining drips of beer into her mouth. It pained me to watch her.

God, is this view beautiful or what? she said, it's just—

There's no view, Jean, I interrupted. It's fucking dark, and we need to go.

The violence in my voice startled me. I hardly ever said *fuck* and felt a new rise of rage at Jean for my ugly impulse to use it.

Okay, she said, finally turning from the ledge, lowering her can of PBR. To my profound distress, she paused yet again.

It was real good to see you, she called to the skinny one, who didn't answer. In the hazy light, his hunched body looked even more strung out and desiccated.

Before Jean could prolong our exit any longer, I started toward the muddy trail and was relieved to hear her shuffling to catch up. Neither of us spoke as we guessed our way through the darkening woods, stumbling over the muddy, uneven stones that were hard to make out now on the dim trail. I couldn't stop listening for the roar of the ATV coming up the path after us. Rigid with panic, I tripped over a crushed beer can and nearly fell. Jean nearly fell, too, over a loose stone or root. It was too dark to even know what we were tripping over.

We should've left earlier, she said.

You think? I continued down the path, trying to make out the vague ground ahead of us. I kept squishing unexpectedly on patches of thick mud I'd thought were just shadows. In the faint, remaining light, the broken chair parts and bottles littering the woods looked threatening and spectral. The sight of Jean's truck ahead of us, the shelter of it, felt as uncertain as the mirage of a lake in the desert until we reached it.

Inside the truck, I locked the doors immediately and blasted the heat, lifting my hands to the vents. There hadn't been much of a breeze on the cliff, the air still warm from summer and full of mosquitoes, and yet I felt clammy now, and cold. I pressed my hands between my knees. When Jean reached over to touch my arm like everything was fine, I pushed her off.

Who was that? I asked her. Why are you telling drug addicts that you're my mother?

She turned on the engine and told me to calm down. While she reversed the truck and got us back on the road, she said he'd lived next to her for a while and he'd just made a guess. My years raising you, she said, must have come up when he was in the house and he just assumed—

Why was that racist psychopath in your house?

He's not a psychopath, she snapped at me. And he's no racist either. He's got a sister who's half Mexican.

So what? I said. That doesn't mean he isn't racist.

And what would you know? she answered. You don't even know him!

But clearly you do, I said. You couldn't get away from him. You completely forgot I was there.

Oh stop it, I didn't forget about you, she told me. I knew you were all right.

Actually, I corrected her, you didn't know. You were wagering with my fucking life to talk to some strung-out man a third your age whose asshole friends talk nonstop about their guns and—

So they like hunting, why should that make them assholes? she said with a hard edge to her voice, driving faster now down the mountain. Maybe your father, she went on, didn't have to hunt deer to feed you, but that doesn't mean—

They didn't talk about hunting deer, Jean. They were fantasizing about shooting someone!

When? I didn't hear anything like that, she said.

Because you were too busy laughing on the ledge, I told her, and weren't paying attention.

It sounds like they were just joking around, Jean said and I sucked in my breath, bewildered at how intently she was determined to deny whose beer she accepted, to pretend there had been no stench of potential violence from the moment the four of them had roared up in their roofless ATV.

I began to yell at her, accusing her of being delusional. Why can't you just admit it, I shouted at her, that they were the embodiment of white supremacy?

Wow, the embodiment of white supremacy, Jean repeated in an oily tone. Give me a fuckin' break, Leah. They didn't do anything to you. All they did was offer you a beer. One of us had to be gracious and accept one. What else was there to do?

How about leave? I wailed. How about get the hell out of there instead of ingratiating yourself to a bunch of homicidal men on a cliff and forgetting all about me?

Stop saying that, she demanded. I've never forgotten about you, Leah, not for one second.

Really? I said. You didn't move out without leaving me a note, or even a number to call you? That didn't happen either, I guess, did it?

Jean started driving more wildly then, causing the truck to rock around the curves in the mountainside, and I felt the muscles tightening in my throat, my whole body sharpening against her.

You know I'm right, I declared. You know you would've gotten nervous if I'd called my husband in front of them and started speaking in Spanish. Or if I was Black, and I asked you—

But you're not Black, Jean cut in again.

Obviously I'm not Black—I'm trying to make a point! What if I'd brought up your Jewish relatives, or all the Jews I come from, what about that? I shouted, exasperated, grabbing hold of the door to avoid hitting my head against the window when we drove too fast into another curve. I'm just making a point, I reiterated, about what lowlifes—

Your dad always used to call people lowlifes, she interjected. And you've got that same air now of superiority, Leah, breaks my heart, to be honest. And what do you know about what low looks like for someone here? When was the last time you were in this town? I'm likely to see every single one of those guys again. You understand nothing here, okay?

I know when someone's staring at my breasts, I told her. I know when they're lewd enough to eye my crotch!

Well, I didn't see any of that going on, Jean insisted. I didn't see anyone bother you, she said, her voice getting louder, and now you're calling me a dirtbag for drinking one beer when—

I never called you a dirtbag, I interrupted, but she shouted over me, letting the truck careen even faster down the mountain. Jean's speech kept coming faster, too, a great rush of fuzzy statements about how much she liked having a Black president, how smart and good-looking he was, and everyone was fine with him, and wasn't that proof that things were getting better, and why was I so stuck on how she handled an encounter with a few idiots on a cliff who had no say in anything in this country, who probably didn't even have bank accounts.

As she ranted on, the grade of the mountain felt like it was falling away entirely, and I stopped trying to interject. I just let her shout on, hoping we wouldn't crash, knowing there would be nobody to find our bleeding bodies for hours, except maybe that same crew of men. At some point, they would finish their beer and come flying down this same road, probably fly right by us, without any idea that they were what we were fighting about, arguing over them with such intensity that we lost all sense of our own survival and struck a tree.

I'll tell you what, Jean said, clenching her hands on the steering wheel, lowering her voice enough that I turned to her, unsure what was coming. She pursed her lips and warned me that I better not tell my father she'd placed me in harm's way. Nothing happened to you on that ledge, she declared. Nothing at all, okay? I didn't forget you were there. And I didn't say I was your mother. I have a few pictures of you in the house and I guess he just assumed—I mean I did raise you for nine years if you recall.

Yes, I do recall, I told her, and you liked it when people called you my mother. You never corrected them.

By that point, the darkness on the mountainside felt terrifyingly close and complete, the night erasing even the trees right outside the window. There was no reflector on the guardrail along the roadside, nothing to indicate where the larger forest began. The world ended with the two beams of Jean's headlights and that was it. Nothing else was visible. With the heat vents still blasting, the truck cabin had become infernally hot, the air drying up my contacts. I couldn't stop squeezing my eyes shut.

Yet neither of us flicked the heat off. I felt too immobilized with anguish to touch anything on Jean's dashboard as she yelled about the need for me to get off my high horse, showing up after twenty years, thinking I knew more about people in this town than she did.

I shouted back that she knew only one of them and was guessing about the rest, that she was defending them just to defend herself for choosing to stay on living here with them. You weren't brave enough to leave with us and you know it, I told her, sucking in more of the dry heat that kept blasting at our faces. You think you're brave but it's not real, I yelled, accusing her of only know-ing how to act brave around assholes, of ignoring me to impress them. I spat on every letter *s*. I'd become venomous and didn't care if I was being cruel. The desire to wound her had become overwhelming. The way you flirted with those men, I told her, was just pitiful. You—

Stop it, Jean demanded with such blunt force that I did stop. I hadn't heard her use that harsh tone with me in so long. She'd used it rarely when I was a child, only in moments of physical peril, when I hid under some bushes at a party and didn't know they contained a beehive. The bees stung Jean all over her face and arms when she crouched to pull me out.

In the truck now, it was startling to hear her use that rare harsh tone to insist she hadn't flirted with anyone on the cliff. She ordered me to knock it off, said I didn't understand what it took to get along here, claimed she'd had to compensate for my standoffishness.

That's what happened, she declared. That's it, and I didn't forget about you either, not for a second. You want to think ev-eryone here is a racist and a psychopath, she said, that's your business. But please don't leave thinking I wasn't looking out for you—that I can't stand for. You have no idea how much I've gone on caring, Leah, she said with such sudden feeling in her voice that a crushing anguish overtook me as well, and fear.

I misjudged your father, she said then. I didn't expect him to be vengeful enough to prohibit you from seeing me. If I'd known he had that in him, I would've stayed, she told me. I would've moved with you to goddamn Jupiter if he'd wanted, and I've waited a hell of a long time, Leah, to tell you this. Could we stop squandering this one visit? Would that be all right with you?

I wiped my eyes and didn't respond. The road had finally delivered us into the valley. Under the first streetlight, a tilted car missing most of its wheels seemed afloat in shadows. Jean turned left onto a wider street leading us past the night-filled windows of one vacant storefront after another, past the deserted town square and a lone hunched-over man shuffling along the dark edge of it in a baseball cap.

At a stop sign in front of a boarded-over shoe store, Jean switched her tone as abruptly as the flick of a light. With an almost maniacal peppiness, she urged me to tell her about living in the Big Apple, if I went to art museums, if I'd seen the Louise Bourgeois exhibit. She'd seen it listed in one of her magazines. She wanted me to know she'd kept her subscription going all these years, that she read every issue. I mumbled a few nonanswers to fill the minutes until we reached the hotel parking lot and this excruciating night would be over, the only night we'd been together in twenty years. It felt deranged, Jean's determination to name exhibits from her magazines, as if every accusation we'd flung in the truck had altered nothing and we could just chat instead about art and museums, pretend we still had a deep sense of each other, when it was obviously no longer true.

You know I've finally started welding, she said at the last red light before the turn into the Holiday Inn parking lot. She told me she drove over to her family's scrapyard, where she picked up free sheet metal to play around.

My house is only a few minutes from here, she said. I'd love for you to take a peek at what I've been working on. I think you'll get a kick out of it.

I just want to get to the hotel, Jean, I told her. Please.

But why? It's not that late. She idled at the intersection after the light changed, cajoling me as if there were no possible reason at all for my reluctance, as if we hadn't just eviscerated each other all the way down the mountain.

C'mon, she said, what's the rush? I thought I was going to get to enjoy you all evening. You don't have to eat my cooking. Just let me show you what I'm welding.

I shook my head, afraid if I answered my voice would crack. I would've gone with her gladly if she'd just left the cliff when I asked, if she hadn't defended those men, hadn't put me down with such a devastating comparison to my father. I'd expected for us to spend the whole evening together as well, had imagined getting pizza and peanut butter Blizzards at the Dairy Queen, reconnecting with such ease that we'd resume our intermittent phone calls now that I was back living in the U.S. I'd imagined planning a second trip for her to meet Gerardo.

But I couldn't let go of the feeling that those men on the cliff were more real to her now than I was.

Just ten minutes, Leah, c'mon, she urged me again, and I told her I would get out and walk if she didn't hit the gas and drive the last block to the Holiday Inn.

You're not going to let this go, are you? Jean asked.

When I didn't answer, she gunned the engine and we began moving again. The silence that last block felt as final as if we'd drawn a physical curtain between us.

She pulled to a stop under the concrete roof over the lobby entrance and I opened my door immediately. I hope you know I'm always here for you, Leah, she told me, and I mean that.

Okay, thanks, I replied, wiping my face as I scrambled out. I didn't turn to wave or acknowledge her again before escaping into the Holiday Inn, relieved at how fast the automated glass doors drew shut behind me. Jean's announcement in the truck about starting to weld didn't stick in my mind. I was too determined to be rid of her, and permanently, to extract her from my psyche for good.

When Silvestre was born less than a year later, I wasn't ready to reconsider. I didn't want my son to know my only experience of a mother was a woman who'd chosen to drink beer on a cliff with white supremacists, with this expressionless young man in a buzz cut who's just risen from her porch step and is now standing less than a foot from my family.

Once I come to a stop beside Gerardo and Silvestre, I recognize the scar on Elliott's chin, the way it continues up through his lower lip. The possibility that he might have murdered Jean in this house feels newly likely. And newly possible, too, that Gerardo's insistence on continuing as we planned, getting out of the car and going inside with Elliott to see Jean's sculptures, might be a mistake. And what for? What chance is there that Jean sculpted anything worth risking our lives to behold, if she would choose to shelter a young man like this, refuse to admit anything unhinged about him, deny the likelihood that he and some of the others in that ATV might show up with their Glocks and shoot her?

Somewhere nearby, a lawn mower drones. Other than that, there's no other reassuring sound of adjacent life. No other cars come down the street. No signs of anything animate except the slight breeze in the weeds and the clumps of high grass taking over Jean's front steps and the broken planks of the other porches all around us. It feels as if I have delivered my family into a ghostscape, like we've become phantoms ourselves, trapped with Elliott amid the stillness of this forsaken place.

Long trip, I guess, Elliott says, and Gerardo tells him yes, much longer than he expected.

JEAN

After Elliott's eviction, I kept clear of my front room. Twice, a skunk came and I sank my mind into the pungency of its smell like a form of penance. I didn't touch any of the long pieces of scrap metal where Elliott had left them on the floor. I picked up my tar paper once and tried to play around. My mind felt too ugly, though, to deserve the pleasure of that kind of fun, folding shapes to find out whether they'd feel new and come alive in my hands.

I didn't want to go small again either. I didn't want to scale down to the meager size of my earlier Manglements, before Elliott. The proof of his time in this house stood in the middle of the room. It was one hell of a totem, erect and phallic, and I didn't step near it. I also didn't do anything about the swelling starting to harden around my incision. I just waited for the pus to rise, for the flesh of my thigh to rot in revolt. The swelling felt like it was speaking for whatever I should have said or done with Elliott, the flaws of my impulses. I waited for the pus like it was a conviction.

A ridiculous man on TV was still peddling lies about the president's birth certificate. In my revulsion at how I'd pushed things with Elliott, I forced myself to keep watching the sick pleasure this greedy man took in pushing things, too. I thought of Steve across the street, likely squandering his day on his parents' old couch watching this same bastard on TV, licking up these bigoted stupid lies like ice cream, and Betsy probably watching up the street as well, in the demeaning little kingdom she kept going in her parents' deli. All my life, I had defined myself against the two of them, and maybe I was kidding myself, thinking I existed on the other side of some partition, with people who were decent through and through.

For a long time, I took in that ridiculous man's garbage talk like a measure of myself. I knew the way the skin was hardening around my incision was a bad sign, too, but I'd lost the drive to do anything but lie there on the couch and replay things in my mind. After the shock on Elliott's face at finding me outside the bathroom, I could have turned things around. I could have finally left a towel for him on the counter. He'd clearly been too nervous about what I was after to just ask for one.

And what had I been after? Not to be some benign grandma with no libido, that was for sure. Louise had refused to deny the libido, the life force of it in herself and her art and everyone else. I couldn't deny mine either. Not when I'd waited so damn long to make my Manglements. I'd thought I could be both. Mostly grandmother, and on occasion a bit wolf.

I'd never expected to produce that kind of dread on Elliott's face, for him to think I was waiting for him to come into the kitchen and grab one of my old tits that way. It was agony to remember. I'd wanted him to find his hours here a refuge. Most mornings, his laugh had seemed genuine, and I'd certainly taught him enough to get some other welding work. At least he had a skill now beyond spitting in the grass, and with his police record he was going to be stuck in the shadow economy for some time. At the hospital, we couldn't hire anyone with a record unless they'd gone a full decade without another incident.

At least I wasn't in the same league of monster as Betsy, paying Elliott's mother with damaged rolls of toilet paper and day-old hoagies. Or maybe I was. Maybe Elliott had only laughed and whistled here to flatter me, same as his mother had surely forced a smile no matter what kind of insulting joke Betsy made about her customers as soon as they stepped out of the deli. And who knew what other wretched arrangements were going on now, behind other closed doors all over the East End, how many guessing games were being tolerated to get a few more dollars from whoever still had a little cash, people convinced they were mostly doing a kindness.

For a few nights, I stopped going upstairs at all. I molted on the couch, hoping to shed as much of myself as I could clicking around online and reading the Van Gogh biography I'd picked up at Bull Creek. I read about his attempt to paint his own face thirty-five times and still finding there was something hidden there that he couldn't reveal. It made sense to me that he hacked his ear off after the thirty-fifth attempt, convinced he was still nowhere near getting it right.

It was a gunshot that finally blasted me out of my stupor. Around three o'clock that Saturday night, four shots cracked the air. The police sirens started up soon after, and a whole hour

later, the wail of our incompetent ambulance. The drawn-out
tragedy went on so long that I gave up on sleep for the night. I
took the last painkiller I had left from the hospital. To calm my
mind, I got some tar paper from the front room. No new shape
formed in my mind, but I went on folding and unfolding the
paper anyhow in the dark, enjoying the familiar thickness par-
ticular to tar paper, how it keeps a fold without much effort at all.

Of their own volition, my hands formed a cube with the paper. I tore off one side, enjoyed the ripping sound in the dark,
sticking my fingers inside, into the emptiness that is a box. It felt
so good I bent more tar paper into another cube, tore off one side
of that box as well, then a third, and stacked them, and it hit me
how I could make a tower on my own if I used the smaller Manglements I already had. I'd just start welding them together.
Maybe I was destined to fail with my Manglements a little longer. I could go to the hospital tomorrow, still do something about
the rotten mess of my leg.

In the dark, I dragged my stiff, pus-filled thigh into the front
room. Only one bulb worked in the ceiling lamp, and in its dim
light, the rise of the tower I'd welded with Elliott had a potency
that felt undeniable, the male shape of it hosting such tiny, wom-
anly capsules all over its sides, the way they invited a closer re-
gard. I ran my fingers over the hard bump of each capsule, tested
whether I knew by memory the diagonal of how they spiraled up
the sides, and I knew. There was something in this world I'd
come to know with absolute certainty—it was the exact distance
between each capsule on this tower. With Elliott, this tremen-

dous sculpture had happened, had come from the same mind as
my ugliest impulses, and also maybe some of the better ones. I'd
intended to be kind, and to his mother, too, when she came asking for water. I'd fully intended to be a mother myself, to help
Leah get wherever she needed to go until the day I died.

I closed my eyes to get rid of the thought, of any thought. I ran
my hands over each Manglement on the shelves, relishing how
well I knew them just by touch—every cockeyed lid, every side
I'd slanted to allow for a little shout of light. With my leg throbbing, I couldn't crouch and touch the larger Manglements down
on the floor. I felt wobbly even leaning against the shelves, and
yet also newly solid, steadier than I had at any point since Elliott
had wedged his knees between my legs in the kitchen, the shock
of him grabbing my tit, that miserable dread on his face.

Somehow, the company of what I'd made, revisiting each box
with my fingers and with my eyes closed, made it easier to believe I was worth something. Worth the drive at least over the
mountain to Hamillville to get the pus drained from my leg.

After swallowing a couple of Tylenol, I sat and took my time
with the rest of my coffee, watched the dawn ready up the room,
sweeping the last shadows into the corners. Once my mug was
empty, I crutched down the porch steps to the truck. The birds
were starting up on the cables and didn't seem to mind that I
was inclined to stay alive a bit longer, weld a little more, a little
higher.

The pleasure of my own company came flooding back once I
got past town into the woods, the clean light coming through the

thinner trees. I felt less fatally dirty myself, making my way over this ridge again, moving through those mountains with their five hundred million years of rocks becoming fossils, same as I would. And yet more trees kept coming up through the fossils, the green smell of them wafting into my truck window, expanding under my ribs.

I got a gentle nurse this time at the hospital. She said little as she cleaned the incision. She just flushed the pus out and explained about the ointments and antibiotics. You would have done yourself a favor, the nurse said, if you'd come in sooner.

Well, I guess I didn't want to do myself any favors, did I? I told her, hoping my cranky reply would put an end to the conversation, and it did. She threw the ointment wrappers into the tall metal trash can and let me go. Once I hit the crest of the mountain on the drive, zipping between the trees, knowing every curve of this road, it felt easy again to think mortality was just a matter of character, that staying alive mostly came down to being sufficiently contrarian in nature.

The next morning, I put on some fresh socks and my work pants. I didn't touch the large sheets of metal still lying on the floor where Elliott had left them. I just puttered a bit, playing around with some stacks of my smaller Manglements, how they might add up to a tower I could assemble myself.

I am not what I am, the indestructible Louise said, *but what I do with my hands*. And what I did with my hands for days was stacking, reaching the same scale I'd reached with Elliott with one useless Manglement atop another, towers of them that were not easy to balance with so many cockeyed lids. I sat on my dusty leather scraps on the floor for days, changing up the order of the boxes, seeing what box might restore the imbalance caused by the tilted lid of the Manglement beneath it. Getting all my funny boxes to stack up without falling was like figuring out some secret I'd been making without knowing it. To focus that way again felt holy.

I tried all kinds of stacks, mixing up the sizes of Manglements that went under and above as much as I could without causing a wobble and a crash. In a few places, I stuck in little flat platforms between the boxes, like the middle bun in a Big Mac. With those stabilizing metal platforms, I could get a little wilder, balancing some of the boxes on their sides, and with their lids off, exposing the inside of each box like a small deserted room. I liked the unease of those sideways boxes so much I added one to each tower, which felt right, as a little reminder of the funny contradiction that was a box—the stillness inside a refuge, except for all the ways it was a void.

To start welding all my smaller Manglements together into towers would never have occurred to me without the weeks I'd worked with Elliott.

It was months before I saw him again, lurking among the slumpers outside the Greyhound station. He wasn't saying a word, just standing there, so skinny he looked like he had no flesh left except for that ugly scar hidden under his shirt. He was a runt compared to the bigger-boned, heftier ones tipping back on their heels and swinging their arms, belonging to nothing but one another. Oh, how I wanted to scream out my window for him to get away from that pack of jackals. To get in my truck and come to the house where I'd feed him, would ask absolutely nothing of him in return.

The light changed and my foot went right to the gas. There was no car behind me, no reason to press down that hard on the gas pedal except that it was such an easy thing to do. Driving right past Elliott like a stranger, the cinnamon bun I'd picked up from the bakery bin in the supermarket lodged in my throat. Against my tongue, the icing on the bun tasted like detergent, a sickening foam working up into my brain.

In my driveway, I felt his empty house watching me and I didn't get out. I stayed in the truck cabin, staring at the high grass in their abandoned yard, at the spot where he'd sat on the porch steps and at the cracked windows on their second floor, wondering why I had made no difference. What a terrible thing to have suggested the shower right then, instead of saying yes, of course I could help them. Four hundred bucks wouldn't have changed my finances. I could have been magnanimous and handed over enough money to cover the deposit and the penalty fee. Maybe Elliott wouldn't be huddling now in that sad squad outside the Greyhound station.

Or maybe he would have ended up there anyway, no matter what I'd offered or how decent I'd been to him in my house. Except I hadn't been decent, and whether it would have made a difference, I'd never know. I'd had the means to let him take what he needed, and I'd gotten greedy. That was the neighbor I'd chosen to be.

The next week, when a new family of renters moved into Elliott's house, I couldn't bring myself to even nod in the mother's direction. She was a Black woman, tall and quiet, with a little boy who pedaled around on a red bicycle that was too small for him, his bony knees hitting the handlebars when he sped up the street. Someone from the city arrived to connect their water and I stayed away from the window, sanding the corners of one of my new boxes, ignoring the ache in my wrist and shoulder, taking extra Tylenol to postpone the pain.

For weeks, I couldn't bear to turn and look at the mother in her glittery blue head wrap, sitting in the same spot on the second step where Elliott and his sister had talked for hours, eating chips together and tapping at their phone screens. I didn't give much thought to what this new renter and her son might think of me, not until I saw them heading into Porter's deli and hoped Betsy wouldn't be her disgusting self and mutter anything awful. The shame hit me then, of letting all these weeks go by without offering them a hello, an acknowledgment of any kind.

The next time I saw the little boy getting off his tiny red bike in their driveway, I stepped onto the porch and shouted over a hello, asked how they were getting along. It was a cloudy day and there was no reason other than caution for the mother to squint at me.

How's the house goin' for ya, everything all right? I asked, hobbling down my front steps, determined now to be a welcoming neighbor, to assure them they weren't living next to a racist jerk like Betsy. I tried to give the mother the largest, most convincing smile possible. Maybe I'd waited too long. She grabbed for her son's arm and pulled him closer.

The house is goin' fine, she said. We were just headin' inside for lunch, excuse us.

Well, enjoy, I told her. Welcome to Paton Street.

When that mother and her little son moved out a month or so later, I watched with heaviness through the front window in the same spot I'd watched Elliott's family after their eviction. I never learned the woman's name or that of her little boy. I hardly left the house after our awkward encounter. The ever bleaker state of things in the East End was getting to me, the gun blasts at four a.m., the sirens at all hours.

One Tuesday morning, an email from Leah showed up. Not her usual mass request for donations, though. It had my name in the first line. *Hi Jean*, her message began. I read the next sentence twice, cracked my jaw to make sure I was in my head. Leah was coming to Sevlick and she wanted me to know this, for us to see each other. To see me. Seated at the kitchen table in my bare feet, I shivered with the joy of it.

You bet I'm in town. I replied right away and then had to stand to get my bearings before I pressed send, make sure I hadn't misread the email. I'd been letting the world bend away, had been putting off any drive that required passing the Greyhound station and the possible sight of Elliott's vacated face among the addicts there, waiting for deliverance to another world.

The arrival of Leah's email felt almost too incandescent to bear. I had to squint at the words like they were spitting sparks.

Her occasional calls in high school, my replies all these years to her mass emails, had not added up to nothing.

I let her know I could pick her up at the Holiday Inn whenever she arrived, that she could stay at my house if she wanted. After a squint, I deleted the part about staying here. She wouldn't be able to leave her dad at the hotel, and I didn't want to scare her off before she even arrived. Before she could come here and see my Manglements. And how could I have left this world without showing her what I'd finally come to make, without her seeing why I couldn't have stayed with her father, allowing him to put me down all day and then crawl on top of me at night?

Although she wouldn't want to hear that part, and she didn't need to. All Leah needed to know was how many messages I'd left for Dave, pleading for him to let me see her, and his merciless decision not to allow me any contact except for cards and letters.

LOVE LOVE LOVE, I wrote and then deleted two of them, keeping only the first. I thought of Agnes, paused my fingers and pictured the calm, sure lines of her grids, her belief in trusting what was known in the mind, and wasn't that equally true of love? Wouldn't Leah know it when I wrote it once?

L!O!V!E!, I tapped out on my laptop, unable to resist a little exclamation for an occasion this momentous. Once I sent Leah my reply, I cleaned every room like the reborn. I had only four days to get this house presentable, and there were plates everywhere. A scummy butter knife in the hallway. Bits of crumbs on the TV. I still couldn't eat in the kitchen without thinking of

Elliott shirtless in the doorway, the tight desperation in his voice when he said *those little fuckin' towels*.

Except I didn't want to think about Elliott now. I wanted to wrap my whole being around the sweet thought of Leah coming back at last. Those random phone calls from her in high school had meant something. She hadn't lost all sense of her early years being my kid, napping best if she put her warm little hand on my arm while I read to her. I'd taught her to use underpants and to read and to take off on a two-wheel bike. Whatever she learned from me, though, Dave would come home and insist there was a slightly better way to teach her.

I hoped seeing Leah on her visit wouldn't mean having to see her goddamn father. In her email, she said they were coming for the funeral being held for her father's friend Fred. I hadn't thought about who Dave might have stayed in touch with here, given the level of his loathing for Sevlick. He'd liked going to the medical library to swap Big Ideas with Fred. It made sense that if Dave was going to come back for a funeral it would be for Fred, who'd been unusual for Sevlick. He'd read more books in a week than most people at the hospital did in a year. If Fred came by with a book for Dave, I was expected to clear out and busy myself reading to Leah. We'd come up with our own Big Ideas upstairs and now, finally, I'd get to find out who she'd become, after all those nights requesting that I keep two voices going, so she'd know when I swapped parts and was speaking as the wolf.

Just in case Leah might want to stay over, I got some fresh sheets for the spare room upstairs. I went in there so rarely I hadn't realized the window had a leak. The mattress had a funny odor, too, and I decided to air it out before putting on the sheets.

In the hallway upstairs, I found a barbecue rib bone that must have slipped off a plate from the dinners I ate now in bed. I hadn't realized how many peanut butter pretzel bits I'd lost track of, reading under the covers. I crouched and looked beneath the bed for the first time in a long while. All sorts of socks and malodorous underwear had found their way under there. Once I was crouching, I got a whiff of the red-checked carpet that had been absorbing spills in my room since childhood. Whatever coffee and milk I'd dripped on it wasn't strong enough to gag over, although it was pretty close. Sixty-four seemed a fine age to roll up the rug of my childhood and haul it to the curb, where somebody was bound to see its potential. Anything in the realm of furniture vanished from the curb within a day.

After hauling the carpet, my arms refused to tidy anymore. And once I was in the front room, the new towers started calling to me. Tend to us, the two unfinished ones begged. They both lacked one or two more Manglements to form a stack as tall as the other towers. None of them stood as high as the totem I'd made with Elliott.

Elliott. I'd seen him once more outside the Greyhound station, looking even thinner and strung out. I'd spotted his mother, too, standing in the line of people waiting to enter the clothing giveaway at the Salvation Army. His mother had on a pair of bright red sweatpants with shiny Disneyland logos sequined up the sides, her face as resigned and dreary as ever, staring at the motionless heads in front of her.

For a second, I thought about pulling up at the curb and offering her a ride once she picked out the clothes she needed. I didn't have anywhere to be. I could have done something instead of driving on. Something more than coming home and stacking more of my tiny Manglements into towers until I got them to balance on their own. The work filled me up like a meal, seeing the scale I could make of those smaller Manglements, getting them welded together and rising over five feet off the floor. I had a whole forest of stacked boxes growing in the front room now. The steel mill downtown might be dead, but all the discarded steel coming into Levy Recycling was adding up in here, pulsing with something. With genius. Ha! Fat chance of that, and without Elliott, I was limited in what I could lift. It was infuriating to be stuck with my own puny strength. I'd been stupid—even out of pure selfishness I should've given Elliott the money.

I'd given up on the casket I'd imagined for my father, or even sticking to the six-sided form of a box. I couldn't pick up those long heavy sheets and move them from where Elliott had set them down. I'd been able to lift the edge on two of them, though, and create a triangle shape. I'd strained enough to make a three-sided pyramid over the third piece of sheet metal Elliott had cut for me.

Even then, welding a triangular casket out of three of the four sheets had been a struggle. The muscle in my thigh around the grinder wound was somewhat functional now, although I still couldn't squat or bear equal weight on both legs. I had to crawl to work that close to the floor, adjusting the two raised pieces of sheet metal until their edges were evenly pressing against each other. To weld the edges together into a triangular peak required the rest of the filler rods I had on hand. I'd have to get over to Bud's Welding Supply to pick up more rods, and also a new tank of argon.

Down on one knee and pushing the welder pedal with my other foot, I made the clumsiest, bumpiest seam I'd welded in a long time. I'd managed to avoid setting the floor on fire, though, so that was a victory, and metal is such a merciful substance. With enough heat and the right machinery, it forgives nearly everything. With the thought of Leah arriving, I ground and sanded down the weld until my arms were too limp for me to do anything but sit and stare and hope I got this visit with Leah right.

At the very least, I wanted this triangular casket done before she got to town. The expanse of the long-tilted sides of its pyramid shape was too vast to fill with my usual eye capsules, which took most of a day to make just one. At Bull Creek, I'd picked up some red enamel paint for model train cars and never used it. I'd just liked the caboose on the paint label and I knew that bright red would look good against the metal of my Manglements at some point. Sitting on the floor now, with Leah in mind and my ass numb from sitting too long, I brushed on red trains of words for Leah, for Elliott and the wolf I'd become with him.

Once upon a time there was a little girl in a forest . . . I painted on.

I stuck to the gruesome classical version, with the wolf ingesting a bellyful of rocks and the huntsman cutting the wolf open to pull the grandmother out, waiting there still alive inside the wolf. *And the wolf dead from the weight of the rocks it had ingested.*

An artist is one who can fail and fail and still go on, I painted for Agnes.

Why don't you do everyone a favor and make dinner for once, I lathered on for Dave, and *At least you have something you give a shit about*, for Elliott.

Oh Jean, I don't know if that's a good idea, I wrote for my reticent, retreating mother.

I got your tools now, bastard, I wrote next and that was for me, this casket no longer being for my father alone—and screw him. I'd devoted enough hours to him already in this house. I was going to die under his roof.

TRIANGULATION OF THE SELF, I painted in thick strokes with the train paint along the whole of one slanted side, going over each letter at least twice.

This caboose red is absurd, isn't it? I wrote on one of the towers next, the words extending up the side of one Manglement and onto the box above it. I painted on more caboose paint, whatever words came to mind, giving myself over to the thrilling free fall of serendipity. I pictured Leah laughing at the line I painted about my father. We would reminisce about all those cardboard tunnels we'd constructed in the basement, how I'd gone on adding boxes long after she went upstairs. I'd gone on chalking the driveway, too, hours after she left for school. It had been exhilarating to continue drawing on the driveway and recognize that I wasn't crawling around with a piece of chalk for Leah's sake. When I added a turret to the roof of the castle I'd drawn for her, it was because I wanted to chalk another shape and because I was happy.

When Leah first arrived in town, we'd have to take some time to get used to each other again. Maybe we could take the trail out to Burton Rock and walk a little before coming back to the house for her to see the Manglements and the towers I was making with them. I'd let her know that these towers wouldn't have happened without her, all those days fooling around with cardboard tunnels in the winter, chalking up the whole driveway in the summer, getting as wild as we wanted, knowing the rain would come at some point, and none of what we made would last.

Oh, we were going to have a good time. Once I had Leah right in front of me again, once we'd caught up a bit, watching the sunset up on Burton Rock, the years we hadn't seen each other would fall away.

LEAH

I'm not mistaken. Elliott was the drug addict on the cliff who Jean had been reluctant to leave. He seems slighter than I remember, and I don't recall him missing his front teeth. I'm certain of his round, pockmarked face, however, and the scar through his lip. His gaze is lucid now, startlingly so, and it occurs to me that there's no reason to assume he's living in Jean's house alone. His friends from the cliff could be staying here as well, could appear the moment we walk inside, laughing in chilling unison at our naivete, still furious about my contempt for them. They could be inside sipping more cans of PBR with its outdated blue ribbon, still eager to brag about who they would shoot if they could get away with it.

To ask Elliott any questions now, when we're already standing together in front of Jean's steps, feels too late and confrontational. Gerardo has already warmly extended his hand. We brought you some chocolates, he says, and tells Elliott about our stop at the café in the plaza, motioning to the box in my hands.

I watch for Elliott to squint or react to Gerardo's accent, which doesn't happen, or at least not in a visible way. At a loss for how to stop the plan already in motion for this gesture of goodwill, I hold out the box from the café. Elliott takes it from me with both hands and mumbles a thank-you, his angular shoulders hunched under his gray shirt. He doesn't seem to have noticed, or maybe doesn't care, how intently Silvestre is staring at him in that manner children do when they hear their parents discussing someone in tense voices.

You can go in, he says. I haven't moved anything. It's all exactly how she left it.

I nod, still unable to bring myself to speak a word to him, to stop picturing the heavyset friend of his who'd made the popping sound of a gunshot with his mouth, and all the sickening occurrences across the country I've watched on the news since then, returning in my mind to that cliff and my silence while they joked about shooting a Black person at their work site.

The present, however, keeps on happening regardless.

Or I am letting it happen, lacking the courage to do otherwise, to tell Elliott I remember him and his racist friends from Burton Rock. I could insist on staying outside to keep my family safe, although to leave without seeing Jean's sculptures would be cowardly, too. Regardless of the direction in which I turn my face, one half of it will be cast in cowardice, and there's no way to resolve, either, how strongly I expect Jean's creations to be a letdown. Despite everything I've revisited about her, all her years subscribing to art magazines, I can't stop expecting her towers to be woefully amateurish, to be junk.

Ahead of me, Gerardo is stepping through Jean's open door in the assured manner with which he steps through every door, taking our son with him, and so I continue with my family, into the house behind Elliott, though I feel obscene, meekly heading inside and pretending that I'm not studying his back for the bulge of a gun tucked into the waist of his jeans.

In my anxious focus on Elliott's back, it takes me a moment to realize the living room is nothing like what I remember stepping into as a child. Jean has packed the room with so many immense piles of metal cubes that there's barely space to move around inside. Hundreds of tarnished metal spikes jut out of the sides of the cubes, which are covered with brightly painted sayings. Some of the towers nearly reach the ceiling. One painted phrase visible from the doorway brings Jean's voice so immediately alive that my face feels hot reading it. *I got your tools now, bastard!*

My eyes sting, and I rub them, assuming it's from the dust we've unsettled on the floor, or from taking in the massive intensity of what Jean has made in here, the elaborate, intricate differences of every cube in size and shape, some of them slanted like trapezoids—also a tower entirely covered with broken pieces of mirror, glimmering spectacularly in the light from the window. *Lay off with the sparkles, Jeanie, nobody wants that girlie bullshit,* another strip of words says along the side of a tower near the window.

Between the mirrored tower and an even taller stack of metal cubes stands the only stepladder in the room. Compared with the sculptures, the ladder looks minor and insubstantial, although it is a large ladder, and I can see how Jean could have lost her footing on its narrow steps while adding spikes to the tower next to it, or painting on more red words. The phrases are so irrefutably Jean—the whole room feels like an incubator of some invented realm that she was building up inside her. Why didn't it occur to me that she might be crafting a fairy tale of her own, a realm as utterly unclassifiable as Jean herself?

And there is something else on her towers that I can't quite grasp, little strange clear-fronted protrusions stuck to the sides of the metal cubes between the spikes. They stick out like little domes and maybe contain something, though from the doorway I can't tell what. To take in all the towers at once feels impossible, the total absence of the dull sitting room I was expecting, the lumpy, sunken chairs, the dusty displays of plates on the back shelves that now contain strange piles of what look like mutilated spoons, and shoeboxes overflowing with the old photos Jean used to cut up and glue onto the birthday cards I couldn't throw away fast enough.

She was working on that one, Elliott says, when she fell.

He points to a tower so tall I have to crane my neck to see the top of it, where a metal circle extends outward like a rusted halo.

Is that a bicycle rim? Gerardo asks and Elliott says yes.

It's just extraordinary, I . . . had no idea, I begin to say but Silvestre interrupts, shouting in Spanish for me to join him in the maze.

There's toys in the windows! he announces, peering into one of the little clear-front protrusions. He urges me to join him. Mami, look, he says, the soldier doesn't have a head, he has an acorn!

Silvestre laughs at this and doesn't wait for me to draw closer. He takes off to see more, darting between the closely packed towers, and I warn him not to knock anything over, to look out for the tower that seems to be tilting slightly and might tip. He darts again without any acknowledgment of my warning, and Elliott reassures me the towers are pretty steady and shouldn't fall. Silvestre calls out that he's found another soldier with an acorn head and I hear Jean in my mind, urging me to lay off, to let my son experience what she made in his own way, to allow him to be as uninhibited among the towers as she clearly was constructing them, as uninhibited as she encouraged me to be when I was her child, urging me to enjoy every hill we biked down together. She'd insist I stop hitting my brakes all the time, to learn how fast the grade of a hill might take me if I let it.

I believe in living above the line, one of the towers says up the side above two initials.

Who's A.M.? I ask.

Agnes Martin, Elliott says. Jean talked about her all the time, her and Louise.

Who's Louise? I ask.

He gives me a questioning look before he replies, Bourgeois.

Gerardo turns toward me then as well, his lips pursed, like he suspects I've hidden something from him. And I suppose I have.

On the wall leading to the hallway, I notice a painting of a girl. It's the only framed, two-dimensional art I've spotted, though with all the towers I can't see what might be hanging on the opposite wall. What I know is that the misshapen head in this portrait is clearly mine. I recognize the kindergarten photo Jean must have used for it, the purple shirt I have on and the orange rubber bands on the ends of my braids. The portrait is quaint and amateurish, doesn't make any sense next to the ceiling-high spike-covered towers that were clearly her calling.

I figured you'd want that, Elliott says and I turn away, wanting a break from his voice, and Gerardo's, too, to just be alone with the bewildering contents of this room. I want to hear Jean's voice.

WHAT'S A STEPMOTHER ANYHOW, I spot in sparkly paint, and I feel Jean's love pinning me to this place, whether I'm willing or not.

How did she make this hole? Gerardo asks, moving closer to a tower with a jagged hole through it at the height of Gerardo's chest. Was it a bullet? he asks and Elliott nods.

I got her a 30-06, Elliott says and explains that's a kind of hunting rifle. He tells us Jean had him drag the tower into the yard so they could shoot it outside.

Sounds like she asked you to do some pretty crazy things, Gerardo says, and Elliott lets out an uncomfortable laugh. He doesn't offer up a single word about what went on in this house between him and Jean. He just keeps vanishing between the massive, tightly packed towers, his skinny body disappearing behind one and then popping up again behind another like a trickster. Or like some sort of elusive Rumpelstiltskin, determined not to reveal anything more than is his intention to reveal.

This one here, he says, appearing now by the far window, this is the first one I helped her with.

Gerardo and I move toward him, the floor creaking ominously, and it occurs to me the towers might be steady but the floor beneath them is not, that the wooden planks we're stepping across weren't intended to resist the weight of what must be hundreds of pounds of metal. To get a sense of their heaviness, I press my palm against what Elliott says was her first tower, which is made not of metal cubes like the others, but of four long pieces of sheet metal, the sides covered with dozens of the porcupine-like metal spikes and Jean's weird clear-fronted protrusions. Up close now, peering into them, I can see tiny cut-up pieces of old photographs. Gerardo asks what the glass front is made of and Elliott points to the discarded heap of old cameras in the corner behind him.

I don't know how she came up with that, Elliott says with a reverence that is at odds with the threatening, volatile person I was expecting.

She called 'em capsules, he says and points out a machine she used to cut a thin metal frame from bits of scrap metal for each capsule, how she had to match the width of the lenses with one of her spoon heads, all of which seems like a tremendous amount of work just to hold a tiny snippet of a photo and a pine cone, and I notice now the various shades of metal in each capsule's frame. I am stunned that I didn't know Jean had it in her to create a concept this elaborate, to follow through on it over and over again. After college, I attempted a few poems, and once a story, but the sense of exposure was too unnerving. To slip a little of myself imperceptibly into the language of others, as an editor, suggesting words for someone else, felt safer yet still creative, still satisfying. How did Jean find the nerve alone in this house to believe otherwise?

It feels like vertigo, experiencing the wonder of all these wild towers alongside my revulsion of Elliott, the shock of being near him again, his body disturbingly close given the narrow spaces between Jean's massive towers, and I can't help flinching a little at his proximity, the thought of his friends insisting in my mind.

Do you think you can do something with her towers? Elliott asks, and Gerardo tells him of course, we will absolutely do something about these massive, phenomenal sculptures.

I tell Gerardo in Spanish that we should discuss what to do later, once we leave. I don't want to talk about what to do with her towers, not yet. I just want to experience them, run my fingers along the slanted rising line the capsules form, the magical way they loop around the four sides of this first tower. Most of the capsules contain old silver gelatin photos of women's feet in worn, mud-covered leather boots. But there are also misty photos of horse hooves, and also a few random capsules filled with shiny particles, some kind of glinting dust. The mix of women's dirty, worn boots among the hooves and particles is humorous but also haunting. What breaks me is the sight of one single capsule that is not a woman's foot but a hand, clutching the pudgy fingers of a toddler, the only capsule with a photo of human contact in the whole spiraling diagonal. The abrupt tenderness of those two connecting hands makes me aware of my own arms slack at my sides, the impossibility of Jean ever grabbing one of my hands again inside her own. I fist my hands against the thought, but that doesn't feel right, not for Jean, not while experiencing her wild towers.

I run my fingers over more of the capsules, close my eyes until I hear Elliott talking again to Gerardo behind me.

There is no separating this fairy tale Jean made for herself from Elliott's presence in this house, her defense of him, her misremembering of the way his friends relished the thought of shooting a Black person who worked with them. Regardless of how coherent and polite Elliott has been since we've arrived, I can't let my guard down, can't bear to exchange any more words with him than necessary, and he is clearly more comfortable addressing Gerardo than me anyhow, to discuss tools and machinery, two men relating to each other, though it was Jean who erected all this and taught him.

Yeah, she learned from her dad, but I think more from YouTube, Elliott is saying now in a joking, lighter tone to Gerardo, who laughs also. And it is funny to think of Jean learning her techniques to build these towers from YouTube. To hear this also makes me terribly sad for her, the loneliness and determination it must have taken, to keep on studying random videos, with no live teacher to help perfect her technique or talk through an idea.

I felt real bad about her laptop, he is telling Gerardo now in a lowered tone, and I turn around to ask what happened to it. Elliott rocks back on his heels, lets out another of his restrained trickster laughs, and says he thought I knew about the break-in. It was four years ago, he says. Just after that time you came to town.

JEAN

I couldn't sleep after Leah's visit, couldn't weld, couldn't get the plumb bob of regret inside me to stop swinging back and forth. No state of stillness would come to me. I couldn't focus on reading, not even Louise. I turned the TV on and then clicked it off. Every sitcom and talk show felt like a dispatch from some realm of humanity that had nothing to do with me. I should have agreed to leave the cliff with her earlier than I did. I just couldn't bear for Elliott to think I wanted to get away from him, that he meant nothing. Leah's clipped, standoffish reaction to him from the second he arrived didn't help either, dismissing him and his friends as vile subhumans to get away from as soon as possible.

Still, I shouldn't have left her standing alone with the other ones as long as I had. A cliff with a crew of drunk men was no place for a woman her age to linger, and there had been something unnerving about the tall one. She hadn't been wrong about the need to leave. I thought I'd tried to apologize. If she hadn't gotten so snide about Elliott in the truck, maybe it would have felt possible to explain a little more. I couldn't bear hearing her

assume that same superior tone as her father, using it to put me
down.

To accept that tone from Leah was like swallowing rancid
lunch meat. My whole being just refused. Who wanted to be
talked to like they were an ignorant piece of shit, and by the
child I raised! I'd taught her how to write her name, to get on her
tiptoes and check out her own books at the library. Didn't all
those hours count for something, measured against just one evening on a cliff that hadn't gone as planned? I should have agreed
to leave when she asked, but did that make me irredeemable?
For Leah to presume she was so morally pure, so above reproach.
Oh, it was just too annoying.

Yet the truth remained that there was nobody on this planet
who I loved more. What was I supposed to do with all that love
for her I couldn't stop, even if she'd written me off as some stupid bigot?

Every afternoon, I reread the last email she'd sent before coming back to town: *Can't wait to see you, Jean!* She'd written that,
had come out of the Holiday Inn with that same earnest expression she'd had as a child, eager to get in my truck and be with
me again. I felt sick about all of it, couldn't stop thinking about
how things might have gone if I hadn't taken her to Burton Rock,
or if Elliott hadn't shown up with his drunk crew. The tall one
seemed absolutely craven, straight out of *Deliverance*. I knew how
to handle him, though. I'd been handling men like him my
whole life. It was Leah I hadn't known what to do with, with her
woman's face and expensive-looking haircut, the irritating re-

serve in the way she spoke. I couldn't stand how she stiffened, as if Elliott had no right to speak to her, like he was some inferior species. And yet who was I to fault her for that, having denied Elliott the simple decency of his own towel?

Oh, I'd never been any good at thinking things through. Leah had scrambled out of the truck like I was poisonous. She hadn't even turned to wave, didn't look back for so much as a second before stepping into the Holiday Inn. For a good week or more, I worked up the nerve each day to press reply to her last email, then just sat and stared at the blink blink blink of the cursor.

I hoped one of Leah's mass emails would arrive and I could donate to one of her causes and we could start over. Maybe she'd keep me in her group emails, and after a little break to cool off, I could wish her well and we could try again. It was a consoling thought, anyway, something to make it easier to get off the goddamn couch, fix an extra mug of coffee, and try to get working again, cut some sheet metal for a new Manglement.

I thought I was mostly okay until I pulled my welding helmet over my face. Under the cover of the helmet, I cried. The most pitiful sounds came out of my mouth and echoed right back against my ears within that small plastic chamber on my head.

Through the dimmer screen in the helmet, I could barely make out the jumbled mess in the room around me, which was a relief. Or a relief at first, until I got dizzy, my ears ringing from hearing too many of my own wretched noises, and I yanked the helmet off. And there they were, my Manglements, with their cockeyed lids and uneven sides, weird, small, probably beautiful to no one else. But I wanted to behold them more than anything in the world. I took off the helmet and stared at them for a long time.

My own company felt easier to bear with my helmet and gloves on, filling the front room with the glow of the weld. The sudden whizzing sound of the band saw. I thought of my father, the solace I'd seen him find in doing this same thing, filling the silence of his days with the loudness of machines doing his bidding. I welded new capsules, got a new Manglement going, went to bed physically spent enough to zonk out for at least a few hours without waking up, agitated, spinning through that disastrous visit with Leah in my mind again. Her insistence on lumping Elliott in with his friends, assuming they were all card-carrying members of the KKK or white nationalists—or no, she'd said supremacists. I'd started noticing the younger newscasters using that word on the TV now, the ones closer to Leah's age.

One night a few weeks after her visit, in the first hours after falling asleep, I woke to what sounded like the creak of the front door. I thought I'd misheard. Even after a soft thump downstairs, I told myself I was just having another fitful night of sleep. Nobody was breaking in. The sound had to be something the wind had blown up onto the porch, some debris from the street thumping against the front door. Except it was humid, a still night, no wind whatsoever, and then the floor planks creaked twice. Three times.

I balled up under my mother's old floral sheets, stared up at the sunken corner of my ceiling, and felt the suck of the void that would be my life if my towers got destroyed, all the delicate capsules I'd welded onto my Manglements. Five years of welding and sawing and working toward the ceiling.

Somebody was definitely down there, had broken through the door, and my body said Elliott—I felt his presence like a heat all over my skin. I held my breath, imagining him getting his bearings in the dark, squinting at my new towers, aching for him to admire rather than destroy them. To just steal whatever he needed and leave my towers alone.

I heard an anxious whisper downstairs and then a male voice that wasn't Elliott's. A jokey, obnoxious voice and I felt a blockage in my throat, realizing I might be wrong and there could be anyone down there.

Shhh, a second male voice said, a softer, more cautious voice, and I felt it then with certainty. Every nerve ending in my body said it was Elliott down there in my front room again. I hoped all that was coming was robbery, no arson, none of them getting off on the idea of coming upstairs and shooting up some old lady in her bed.

I hoped the other male voice down there didn't belong to the tall one who'd been on the cliff. There had been something really off about him. Elliott would know where to find my purse, in the kitchen next to the toaster. He'd know where my laptop would be charging on the kitchen table. For him to take the copper pipes out of the bathroom seemed fair enough.

I pictured his face downstairs in the dark, vacated and wasted-looking, his gaze rubbed out by whatever he was swallowing now or injecting. At Burton Rock, he'd looked close to erasing his very being.

Something metal clanged downstairs. Not a heavy clang, not one of my towers pushed over. Elliott wouldn't destroy anything I'd made—unless he would.

I pictured his face downstairs, the scar through his lower lip that had become so familiar, his unwashed carpenter jeans cinched like the pants of a scarecrow and under his shirt that thick, raised scar on his chest, the shock of it when he'd come into the kitchen. My head ached with the strain of trying to hear some sound downstairs to be unmistakably Elliott.

A male voice that was not Elliott's let out a drunk, nervous laugh. Some kind of destruction was sure to come. My chest hurt waiting for it, recalling how rabidly I'd defended them to Leah just because Elliott had been among them. I sure hoped that heavyset friend of his wasn't down there, too.

A rolling sound began below—one of my emptied paint canisters, I guessed, moving across the wooden planks of the floor. I'd thrown out most of the empty bottles, although a few weren't empty yet and were probably lying around the workbenches. I pictured one of Elliott's unlaced construction boots kicking one of my emptied paint canisters in the dark, causing that rhythmic rolling sound over the planks of the floor.

After another nervous whisper, there was a long silence and I let my mind sink again into the version of what was going on downstairs that was easiest to bear alone in my bed, of Elliott feeling something down there beyond anger and resentment. For him to be recalling something of his curiosity for what I was up to, whistling in here as he worked on the finished tower still standing where he'd left it, next to the window. I held on to the thought until it became an ache in my shoulders and down my neck, my whole back willing Elliott to pause down there in the dark for just a second and take in what I'd made, for him to notice how I'd stacked all the smaller Manglements to keep on working at the larger scale he'd helped me reach.

I closed my eyes to figure out which of the creaking sounds might be his. Hadn't I known him? Hadn't we reached some kind of genuine connection, even if I'd quietly gone about screwing it up? It occurred to me that I would rather be shot outright than have to lie here and listen to them push my towers over, or piss on them just to get each other laughing and prove my art was nothing. That we were all nothing.

For a long withering time, I lay in bed, aching for Elliott to finish taking whatever he thought he needed here to survive, hoping he hadn't resigned himself completely to that crew of idiots. I hoped he was feeling something down there in the dark at the sight of my towers, beyond a desire to pick up a hammer and destroy them.

After more nervous whispering, I sat up against the headboard, uncertain if I was more likely to save my art by staying in bed, pretending I was asleep. I could go down and warn them the police were on their way and see if that scared them off—if that would scare them, that is, instead of provoking them to clobber me with a hammer. Or shoot me dead.

Elliott knew the houses on either side of me were vacant now, and vacant across the street, too. He knew that absolutely no one would hear if I cried out.

I heard the front door creak again, an end to the whispering.

For a while, I listened to an owl hooting in some tree nearby, the steadying repeat of its reedy call. I didn't pay much attention to bird sounds, not unless I was approaching hopeless and needed to fixate on something that felt like a sign of mercy.

Until the first poke of dawn at the window, I didn't dare head downstairs. Whatever was missing down there, I didn't want to find it in the dark. I waited for the light to reach into the familiar sunken corner of my bedroom ceiling. To be breathing in this room, not a corpse yet, felt extraordinary. A minor miracle to get up once more, leave the bed unmade, move through my open door into the soft square of light from the hallway window and then the long rectangles of light coming through the loose wooden banister along the stairs. It was soothing, the familiar creak of my old feet landing on each step, the familiar absence of any other sound in this house but my slow self.

In the front room, my towers were in the same semicircle, just how I'd left them. Still standing crooked as cacti and looking more delicate to me than I remembered, each jagged stack of boxes rising with its own tenuous balance. They looked newly vulnerable to me, cactus-like in shape but without any of a cactus's thorns for self-protection. Some heavy railroad spikes might fix that, and they would be easy enough to find at Bull Creek. I could add a whole bunch of those old railroad spikes on every side. I saw it in my mind immediately, and how fun it would be to weld them on.

Wouldn't that surprise Elliott if he broke in again, to find those sharp spikes on every tower. If it was Elliott who'd come last night, and who else would have carefully moved between these towers in the dark instead of knocking them over? None of my tools had been taken, not even the plasma cutter.

What they did take was my laptop. My cell phone and wallet. Also the full carton of milk from the fridge and the new bag of Herr's red hot barbecue chips that had been on the counter. Elliott loved those barbecue chips, and whoever had come last night had not gone into the downstairs bathroom, or at least hadn't stolen the copper pipes in there, or from under the kitchen sink either.

Once I got a cup of coffee in my system, showered, and used the landline to cancel my credit cards, any doubt I had about getting right back to work was resolved. What did I need a laptop for anyway?

Agnes Martin hadn't needed a laptop. She'd gone off the radar entirely and on purpose. She'd hung her days on nothing but the silver cord of her own vision and discipline. Whatever technical prowess I'd lacked and could glean from clips on YouTube I'd mostly seen already. And if I really needed to look something up on Weldporn or TIG Time, I could drive over to the public library in Hamillville, or get a new phone.

I'd be okay for the next day or two. Or far longer. To be stripped of any connection to the internet for a short spell might be freeing. I had the landline, and who was calling me anyhow? Who was going to email? Not Leah, not for a good while, I was certain of that. There was no real hurry to replace my devices. To be robbed clean of them seemed as good a reason as any to give myself over to a new tower, to stack up the Manglements I had left on the shelves, maybe make a trip tomorrow over to Marty's scrapyard for some more sheet metal to weld a new larger box as a solid base for this new metal cactus. And once I got some cash out at the bank I could head to Bull Creek to search for railroad spikes.

For breakfast, I ate some stale pretzel rods while I went through the Manglements still on the shelves, thinking about how to balance the remaining boxes in some unexpected way that wouldn't cause them to topple over. It had been over a year since I'd looked closely at the slant of some of their lids and what I'd trapped in the capsules I'd welded onto their sides. I was surprised how immediately I remembered not only what I'd placed in each capsule but where I'd found it—the plastic soldiers I'd picked up at a garage sale over in East Sevlick. The tintype photo of a shy-faced bride I'd found at an estate sale outside Hamillville. A tiny cast-iron goat I'd found on a table full of miscellany at Bull Creek.

Oh, was I glad to still have that funny little goat. I'd been so pleased to find it, though it barely fit under the curve of the camera lens. I'd had to make a wider metal frame that bulged a bit to accommodate the poke of its horns. I'd thought of Leah when I picked up that goat, how much she would have delighted in the tiny size of it when she was a girl. Even if she never wanted to see me again, she was still in these towers, all those afternoons together, coming alive to the freeing pleasure of presuming we could experiment with cardboard however we wanted until her father got home.

And what did it matter if this next tower had no more Art to it than the one I stacked last week? According to the great Louise, I didn't need the world to tell me whether I was any closer to making a new kind of beauty with my towers. I just had to keep getting on the ladder and welding a little higher, withstand a little more. All I needed was railroad spikes.

I would make it clear to Elliott and whoever else might break into this house what they were up against. I'd outfox them. I'd outwolf them. I'd meet them with iron, spikes, train paint, maybe a little gunpowder.

All afternoon I wrote up and down my towers until I ran out of red paint. My mind felt shiny with intention.

I MEANT WELL, I SWEAR, I wrote all up one side.

I WANT TO BELIEVE IN SOLITUDE AND THE GLORY OF MY INNER HORSEFACE, DON'T YOU? I added to the fourth tower because I felt like it, and because if I didn't work up a reason to laugh at myself I would surely become as unmovable as stone and die.

Horseface, I said aloud just to hear something against the silence, to laugh at my own voice until I had to wipe my eyes.

That Saturday after the robbery, I left for Bull Creek at dawn, feeling a bit like a robber myself, creeping out of the house in the pitch-dark. With my phone stolen, I didn't know what time it was exactly when I ducked outside, only that it was dark enough for the moon to give a little glow to the dew on my dead lawn, and on the other dead lawns along the street. I was glad to be finally driving out of here, away from Steve's enormous paranoid sign about shooting trespassers. Away, too, from the X-ed up boards over Alvina's windows on the corner, and over the windows and doors of the houses after that, one grim X after another all the way down the block. Condemned, condemned, condemned, the houses murmured as I drove on faster down the empty road. It was energizing to get away from my own robbed house and this whole dying street and be up on the mountain, to see nothing but trees and the dawn silvering over the ridge.

Driving up past the beer depot and the stoplight still busted before Troy Road, I sat back a little more into my seat. There was some relief in the justice of Elliott cashing in on my phone and laptop, and how could it have been anyone but Elliott who'd broken in? Who else would go looking for the barbecue chips next to the toaster, or would know where along the kitchen wall next to the microwave I charged my phone at night?

Even the thought of Leah, of likely never seeing her again, felt easier to bear, heading back to join the pickers of Pennsylvania at Bull Creek. I hadn't gone to the flea since the grinder accident, and I felt unlocked and alive, imagining all the other pickers driving over this same ridge, sipping from their own cruddy travel mugs as the light rose. I missed the nervy energy of the diehards scanning the tables with their flashlights before the bigger crowds arrived, the jewelry pickers who upsold their finds on eBay or at the higher-end flea markets closer to Pittsburgh. It felt good to think of them all slurping their coffee, making their way to Bull Creek in this same dark, bracing for the screwballs who always showed up, too, hunting for cheap nudie photos and ammo.

I downed my Folger's to the very grains at the bottom and flicked the radio on, punching through the stations for something good until I found Marvin Gaye singing in that exuberant voice of his. Sexual healing, I murmured along, then shouted along—why the hell not? There was nobody on this road to stop me. Sexual healing! I shouted and wished the thought of Elliott would just leave me already.

To get a break from my own mind, I turned up Marvin until my ears rang. I hoped I was still worthy of some minor serendipity in this world—at least some cheap railroad spikes. A canister of model train paint for cheap. Maybe I was asking too much of the universe. Just to pull into Bull Creek without a crash would be nice. I was having a harder time than I used to, seeing where the curve of the mountains tightened in the dark. My night vision had never been a problem before. Even squinting didn't help.

I hit the gas harder up the mountainside anyhow. I'd have to die somewhere in these mountains—maybe it would be on this one. The sun was nearly up by the time I reached the high grass in the parking field for Bull Creek. Dozens of trucks and cars had already filled up a first row, likely the cutthroat crowd who'd arrived last night and slept in their vehicles to peruse the tables this morning before anyone else and get the best deals.

A man in a Penguins hockey cap was waving and directing people where to start the next row. Some veteran flea hagglers still had their flashlights on, their necks extended like birds', ready to peck at whatever the early vendors were putting out. With my wallet gone, I hid some cash for the flea market in my bra. My bigger bills, though, in case I found something great, I zipped into a hidden waist pouch that Dave had bought for me early on. His gifts were always practical, indisputably rational in nature. Yet here I was, more than twenty years later, still using this damn waist pouch.

I spotted one bug-eyed picker who'd been coming for years, her saggy cheeks looking ghoulish in the glow of her flashlight. I didn't recall her looking quite so run-down last spring when I was making my rounds at Bull Creek regularly. A little girl darted up and grabbed her hand with the familiarity Leah used to grab mine with until I lost hold of her—she'd grown up without me, and there was no undoing it. To hear how she remembered my leaving had been scorching. If we hadn't run into Elliott at Burton Rock, maybe that one visit with her would've ended with a showdown regardless, both of us shouting, Leah fleeing without a goodbye, the way I'd left her.

It hadn't occurred to me until she said it in the truck that I could've left her a note. I should've written something for her, though I hadn't intended to leave for good. On the phone that morning, Dave had called me asinine and abruptly hung up on me, same as he always did. He never hung up that way on anyone else, and I called him back just to threaten him that I might leave, to startle him into remembering I didn't have to put up with his bullshit. When Dave didn't answer, I started yanking open my drawers, chucking clothes onto the bed. I assumed he'd want me back for Leah's sake. I didn't expect him to get so vengeful on the phone, accusing me of having a personality disorder. He made it more than clear that he had no interest in a reset, no intention of letting me see Leah again for even one last

Blizzard together at the Dairy Queen. And what could I do about any of it as a stepmother? Nothing.

Getting out of the truck in the dark field, I slipped and had to grab the door handle to catch myself. The ground was hidden lower under the high grass than I expected. I had to poke my toe around. It was like stepping into some kind of abyss, searching with my sneaker to find where the ground was waiting underneath, and all the deer ticks with Lyme disease likely waiting, too.

The vendor closest to where I'd parked was arranging jars of glass marbles. He was a round, balding man, ordinary except for the pizzazz of the chunky brass buttons on his gray sweater. I'd never seen a male vendor at Bull Creek wear any funny brass buttons like that. He kept stepping back to adjust the height and angle of the jars on his display shelf and I moved closer to see if he was trying to offset a broken hinge on his shelf.

Once I stopped to watch him, it was clear what all his slight adjustments were about, what he was intent on doing and how few seconds it would last. He was shifting the height of the shelf and the glass jars to best catch the sunlight moving through his marbles and the small pockets of air between them. After his next tweak, a jar of translucent green marbles caught the light in such a divine way the marbles lit up from within.

You got it, I told him. You made it happen.

He turned around in his gray sweater, a stinging wariness on his long, plain face, like he thought I was making fun of him.

I mean it, I told him. What you're doing there, with the light moving through those translucent marbles, that's sublime. That's Art. You made it happen, thank you.

LEAH

There is just one sculpture lying horizontal on Jean's floor. Its shape brings a mountain to my mind, the way the two pieces of sheet metal lean into each other, forming a peak. Silvestre is crouching beside it, asking me to crouch with him, to tell him what the red letters spell out on Jean's sculpture, and I do. It's a relief to sink to my knees next to him, instead of remaining on my feet with the news that Jean was robbed. I'd assumed the silence after I fled Jean's truck four years ago was chosen and mutual. It never occurred to me that she might not have her laptop anymore. Even if I'd gone ahead and included her on the email announcement about Silvestre's birth, she wouldn't have received it. She wouldn't have known he existed anyhow, that the only encounter they will have is this one—Silvestre running his fingers over her capsules and spikes, the slight openings on the slanted sides of her metal cubes.

And were you in the house at the time, Gerardo is asking of Elliott behind us, when the robbery happened?

Oh yeah, I was definitely in the house, Elliott replies, and I swivel around on my knees to look at him, try to decipher from his expression what he means, but he slips once more behind

Jean's mirrored tower in his unnerving flickering way, his movement altering what shines on the bits of mirror glinting in the
light from the window.

Yeah, Elliott says after an awkward pause, half concealed now
behind the mirrored tower. I wasn't doing too good then, and
Jean knew that. She let it go.

Let go that you robbed her, is that what you mean? I ask.

I helped her make her art, didn't I? She didn't have nobody
else, and she didn't make no will neither, Elliott says, something
shifting in his voice, from the politeness he has maintained until
now into a more defensive tone, and I get up immediately from
where I'm crouching next to Jean's sculpture long as a body on the
floor. I grab hold of Silvestre's hand and yank him up with me.

You mean she didn't leave this house to you? I ask and Elliott
shakes his head.

Nope, he says. And she didn't leave them towers to you neither. She didn't leave them to no one.

So you completely lied then, on the phone, about Jean's will, I
say to confirm I'm grasping what he's just admitted, and Gerardo
warns me in Spanish to be careful.

You don't need to be careful, Elliott says in English. I know
what cuidado means. I don't know everything yins are saying,
but I know that.

His pitted cheeks have started reddening and I feel my own
face getting warm as well. I apologize, tell him I had no idea he
spoke Spanish. The floor creaks then and I can't tell where the
sound is coming from, if it's from my nervous step backward to

stand closer to Gerardo, or if something else has shifted in the house.

It occurs to me that the sound could have come from the hall or upstairs. Or somewhere below us. I get frantic, disoriented, as intensely as I did in college, when I'd lose all sense of what floor or building I'd just entered. If Elliott could rob Jean, invent a will to lure us here, isn't it possible he intends to rob us as well, or worse? Perhaps it wasn't paranoid, my initial fear outside, that one of Elliott's homicidal friends from the cliff could be living here, listening to us from the second floor right now.

My mind whirs with the possibility of Elliott's whole rabid crew about to descend the stairs to retaliate on his behalf, thundering down with their half-finished cans of PBR and their Glock pistols. Maybe Jean isn't even dead and the invention of her fatal fall from the ladder will be Elliott's next revelation.

Except Jean doesn't descend the stairs. Elliott's crew from the cliff doesn't come thundering down either. Nothing creaks again, or not that I hear. For all I can tell, Elliott's subsisting here on his own seems to be true. We remain just the four of us in the front room, Jean's elaborate, spiky metal towers rising to the ceiling around us. Their silent enormous presence, the boldness of them, has begun to feel contagious and I decide to go ahead and ask Elliott what I want to know, why he lied about the will.

I just thought it could help, he says with a shrug.

Help what? I ask.

He lets out a sound like I've asked something obvious. For you to drive out here, he says. Jean got real tense if your name came up, but she had your number on four different Post-its in her kitchen drawer. She had it at the front of her address book. She had your number all over. I thought, I don't know . . . that once you saw what she made, you'd get it.

Well, we do, we get it, Gerardo says, and to my relief he also tells Elliott we need to go, to check into our hotel and make sure there is a cot set up for Silvestre. He assures Elliott that we will be back in the morning, to take more pictures and figure out what we might do with Jean's towers, to give them a life beyond this house.

Elliott nods at this, moving toward the wall with Jean's portrait of me. He asks if I want to take it with us now, just in case we don't come back, but he doesn't wait for me to answer. He goes ahead and unhooks the small canvas from its single nail, and despite everything that has occurred to the contrary, I can't stop bracing for Elliott to get indignant and do something unexpected and terrible.

I watch with dread as he takes the portrait of my girlhood face off its one nail, exposing a glaringly clean square of wall behind it, exempt from the film of accumulated dust and buildup that has discolored the rest of the wall. Amid the gradations of grime, the newly exposed square has a startling emptiness, bright and blank.

It's you, he tells me. You might as well take it.

JEAN

THREE YEARS BEFORE

Deep into January, I woke to somebody jimmying the door again, more creaking from downstairs. Somebody's feet treading across the front room, trying to step lightly, same as the night of the robbery. I didn't hear any nervous whispering this time, though, no drunk laughter, and no more footsteps after those first few creaks of the floorboards.

I thought maybe I'd misread the sounds. For a good hour after the door creaked, all I heard was the wind cutting against the roof and I fell back asleep. In the morning, I didn't find anything new missing—not that there was much left to take. There was no laptop to steal anymore, no cell phone. Only twenty bucks in my wallet.

I didn't know what to brace for when the door creaked again the next night. The cold kept coming harder that week, with thick ice lacing over the windows and freezing in drips along the sag of the power lines, rimming the lower edges of the branches of the trees. I'd been working long days on my eleventh tower. Something in its nature didn't want to comply with my designs for it as the others had. That second night the door creaked, I just didn't have the strength or nerve left to go treading down the cold stairs to see what the hell was going on.

On the third night, when the door creaked yet again, I sensed Elliott as strongly as if we were breathing again on opposite sides of the bathroom door. I sensed his ambivalence about returning to my house, how near frozen he must be to come sneaking in like this at night, to get warm and thaw for a few hours in the dark, hoping I wouldn't hear him, or that if I did, I would leave him alone, let him take the brief refuge he needed.

To see if I was right about what was going on, I stopped sweeping the floor in the front room. I wanted to see if I could catch his boot prints once the metal dust and the soot from the welding smoke on the floor got thick enough. With eleven towers and all of them barbed now with railroad spikes, there were only a few routes through the front room wide enough for a person. The eleventh tower had gotten larger at the bottom, given its refusal to stand on its own and comply with the stability of the others. I'd added a ring of extra support and still it kept tipping when I pulled away the ladder it was leaning against. It seemed to be holding out for some plumb line I couldn't find, some need in its nature I couldn't grasp.

I'm watching you, I muttered to the eleventh tower as I backed away. Either we were going to figure each other out or that tower was going to tip and clobber me. I lacked the strength to break it apart, and dismantling didn't feel right anyway. We'd been staring at each other all winter. You know what Louise would say about you? I asked. She would say you're some kind of mirror, and maybe you are.

From talking aloud, I started coughing. The dust building on the floor to catch proof of Elliott tracking inside was making it harder to breathe. With the windows closed, the dust and metal grit on the floor had accumulated so fast and thick that I could feel it filming over my teeth. I cracked the window, but then I had to deal with the blast of cold stiffening my fingers and shoulders. Annoyed and shivering, I gave up on figuring out what that eleventh tower wanted from me. I heated a can of Chickarina soup for lunch, ate it out of the pot, and lost my focus for the day. I collapsed on the couch for a nap and for a second I thought I smelled Elliott on the armrest and on the cushions, too, his sweat and that pungent Elliott odor of his, like old mushrooms left too long in the produce bin.

The next morning, I crouched and looked closer at the dust leading to the TV den. There were faint prints and they were boot shaped. I got on my knees to really look at them, make sure they weren't just my own overlapping shoe marks, and they didn't appear to be. These prints were definitely wider and larger. They had the broad curve of construction boots. Elliott was returning here to sleep, and alone.

I thought about leaving him a note, letting him know he didn't need to sneak out in the morning before I came down. I held back, though, unsure whether that kind of invitation might scare him off. I didn't want to make him nervous about what more I might expect from him in exchange for his nights staying warm on my couch. Having already forced him to guess what I was expecting him to satisfy, there didn't seem much leeway to explain that this time I was really only thinking of his needs, not my own, which wasn't true anyhow. I was desperate for him to stick around, to have his company and help again.

February snowed on, the ice thickening over the windows. I swept up the dust so I could breathe again while I tinkered with the balance of the eleventh tower, how to get it upright without the support of my father's old ladder next to it. I started hearing the faucet come on in the kitchen at night, and in the morning there would be Elliott's water glass drying on the rack next to the sink. I left his glass on the rack exactly in the spot where he'd left it. He never took any food from the fridge that I noticed. Whatever gradual agreement we had silently come to abide went on into March, sleeping on separate floors, never seeing each other directly.

One subzero afternoon, I came in with my groceries, too frozen and stiff to bother taking off my wet boots. The tips of my fingers stung from the cold and I decided to unload the bags first in the kitchen. I knew the squeak of my wet boots meant I'd have to run a paper towel over the drips later, once I'd thawed, rubbed the cold out of my face and my bad leg. I'd been coming down this hall for sixty-six winters, didn't think about being older and clumsier until I lost my footing, my wet boots flying out from beneath me, my head smacking the wall.

I reached out to catch myself, knocking the hall mirror to the floor, where it shattered with a strange clicking sound. Still lying on the floor, a little dizzy from smacking the wall, I leaned over and saw the mirror had cracked into curiously large pieces that remained in the frame. They were all fingerlike slivers. I'd never seen a mirror crack in such long, jagged shapes. Maybe it was the cold draft in the hall. Whatever the cause, I saw it immediately, how those fingerlike mirror slivers would look if I staggered them up the sides of the eleventh tower like the moving ripples of a creek.

Shaken, cold, my head throbbing, I stayed there sprawled on the floor a long time, staring at the slivers, before I finally took off my wet boots and rose, wobbly, in my socks. After two Tylenol for my various new aches, I sat back down on the floor to mess around with the slivers, see what jagged logic I could arrange with them. It was such a welcome satisfaction, to have absolute control over the shape of something. I rotated the shards until they started talking to one another and insisted I get out of the way. By that point, I was too sore to go out for a glue gun. In case Elliott might arrive and track through the hall in the dark, I arranged the slivers flush against the wall, where he was least likely to step on them.

In the morning, the slivers were still in place, lined up exactly as I'd assembled them, and I felt a rush of goodwill toward Elliott, and toward Donny, who ran the only remaining hardware store this side of the ridge, and who still opened at eight a.m. sharp. Donny was in his usual spot, leaning his big gut against the glass case where he displayed the muzzleloaders and percussion rifles that kept him in business. It was astonishing that nobody had come in and shot him yet, to break into that case.

Glad you're still kickin', Don, I told him.

You, too, Jean, he replied, hobbling toward the back shelves to show me the one glue gun he had left. The plastic packaging was grimed over with sticky crud, though the glue gun looked sturdy enough under the plastic, and Donny had two sets of refill sticks, which I bought, too. I didn't want to lose the morning driving over the ridge to the Target outside Hamillville, and a light snow was starting up.

When I got home, I took off my boots in the doorway to avoid slipping again in the hall. The snow was already banking against the windowsills, its flake-by-flake insistence the perfect company for the slow one-by-one of placing each sliver, gluing them in the same arrangement up the sides of the tower.

By noon, the snowfall gave way to a cold, clean light. The bright beams coming through the window ignited the bits of mirror like they were lit up from inside, like those translucent marbles at Bull Creek. If the tower hadn't been resting against my father's ladder, the sun wouldn't have illuminated any of the fingers that way, guiding my choices about what to glue where. If that tower hadn't defied my intentions, if it had remained erect as readily as the others, I would have gleaned nothing from the sun on how best to puzzle on each sliver of mirror.

To keep on learning is the real secret, Louise said. At least that one secret was within my grasp, even if I'd had to smack my head against the wall to get to it. I had a fantastic time gluing on the shards, angling them to refract the light. The splinters of glass that kept embedding in my fingertips got distracting, and painful. I ran out for some rubber gloves at the Dollar Bargain, and stocked up, too, on Progresso soup and string licorice, some backup canisters of coffee and ginger snaps.

Once I stuck my provisions away in the kitchen, I slipped on my new rubber gloves and took my rip hammer into my parents' room upstairs. There was nobody looking in their big mirror now, over the dresser, no reason not to smash the hell out of it. The mirror was too unwieldy in size for me to take off the wall. I had to smash the face of it where it was, hanging over the dresser. My first whack was too weak to cause even a single crack. I felt too aware of my mother's presence, her shadow in there cringing at me, swinging a hammer against her bedroom mirror. She hadn't experienced much happiness in that room with my father that I knew of, and yet it was still the mirror where she'd relaxed at night as best she could, smearing on her face creams.

I had to close my eyes and block out the thought of her to swing the rip hammer without holding back. In two blows, eyes shut, I hit the mirror with everything I had. The second time, it shattered spectacularly, jagged shards falling over the top of the dresser and onto the floor. Maybe the larger size of the mirror was the reason the shards came flying out, or were responding to the blunt force of my determination, shutting my eyes and hammering my dead mother's mirror into oblivion.

Sorry, I said aloud, still sensing her in the room, her shock at her daughter sweeping the pieces of her bedroom mirror into a plastic bucket. That big mirror hadn't reflected anyone in years. To reconfigure it seemed better than leaving it in here, reflecting no one.

I hope you understand, I said to my mother, in case she was listening somehow, and then I shut the door on that dreadful room. My intentional shattering of her mirror with the hammer didn't result in the elegant long finger shapes of the first one downstairs that I'd broken by accident. With the hammer, I'd ended up with an uneven lot of shards, some large, others minute and sharp even through the thick rubber of the gloves. I used the sharp smaller bits anyhow, gluing a spiral around the tower as high up as my new supply allowed, enjoying the surprise of how each sliver took the light from the window a little differently.

I liked the determined woman, too, staring back in every piece I glued on, the bullheaded hardness on her old soft face, how unafraid she was to break whatever she needed to proceed. She reminded me a little of Louise's ferocious expression in her later years, working on her cells, when she decided she was ready for an entire human-size room to convey the scale and fury she was after.

The shards weren't enough to cover the whole tower. I thought I'd have to head to one of the indoor flea markets over in Deerfield to buy up more old mirrors. To haul a bunch of heavy mirrors to the truck and then into the house wouldn't be easy. I couldn't leave this tower half covered though, not when the mirrors had worked out so magnificently. It was so defeating, to be limited again to what I could carry up the front steps. I slept in fits the next two nights, my legs restless and agitated.

Then Saturday morning I came down and found four bathroom-size mirrors leaning against the wall. I couldn't think how else they could have gotten there except Elliott.

A little gift from Hounslow, well how about that, I said aloud.

The mirrors he'd brought were old, in worn wooden frames, and I hoped he'd pried them off the bathroom walls of some condemned house nearby.

Wherever Elliott got those four mirrors, I was grateful for their arrival. I slipped on my rubber gloves and got smashing again with my hammer, gluing more slivers on the higher boxes toward the top. With the tower still leaning on the ladder, it was a gamble to climb up the rungs, but it was exhilarating, too, knowing I was willing to lose my life this way, fatigued on a ladder, my arms begging for a break, wanting to glue on just one more sliver, to get one more shard in just the right spot. Why had it taken so long to figure out, what kind of careful work would bring a happiness so full and deep that doing it just one minute without falling off a ladder would feel like a gift?

I woke to gunshots that night, more blasts in a row than I'd heard in months. In the morning, the local news reported four young men dead in a condemned, vacant house on Ohio Street, just a block down. I kept watching to make sure Elliott wasn't among them. Drugs is what the news said. Utter desolation is what the faces said when the local news shared close-up photos, none of them Elliott. I read their last names aloud, to relish the relief of them not being Hounslow. Still, once I got sucked into the updates about the four of them dying one street over, I couldn't stop thinking about all those bullets in their strong, young bodies, and about the alloys of bullets, their soft core of lead wrapped in something shinier—copper or steel.

I got to thinking so much about that hidden lead under the

steel casing of bullets that I knew I was going to have to buy some, hold them in my hands. I was going to have to shoot one of my towers and see what the blast of a bullet would add. I thought about the wound Louise had added to her sculpture for Catherine Yarrow, with that rusted nail hammered at the level of the heart.

I worked faster gluing on my bits of mirror after that, eager to move on, fitting on the slivers no longer a novelty, the repeated process now feeling as tedious as dish washing. My mind had already tipped over to how and where to shoot a new tower. Meanwhile the mirrored one still wouldn't stand erect, and the sight of it leaning against the ladder each morning started to drain my sense of purpose. I stopped working and it was disturbing how good a whole day on the couch watching movies felt, to start thinking maybe this was it for me and my foolish attempts at Art. It wasn't like anyone would care, or notice, if I didn't make another tower, if I just grew limp as a human cushion in front of the TV. I made sure I didn't spend the night there on the couch, though, in case Elliott snuck in for a few hours of sleep.

A few more days went on this way, my sense of surrender deepening until I came down in the morning and found Elliott sitting on the floor near the front door. He had his puffy coat on, his knees drawn up to his chest.

I stopped where I was, still on the stairs, shocked at how diminished he looked, like his entire face had fallen in. And his neck was visibly dirty. Some streak of crud running up toward his ear. More crud under his chin. He had more hair than I'd

ever seen on him, too, uneven, patchy stubble over his jaw and on
his head. His stringy dark hair was hanging in dirty clumps and
had grown long enough to tuck behind his ears.

Good to see you, Hounslow, I said, and he nodded, still seated
and crumpled, his back to the door, the familiar flush I'd learned
to look for rising in his cheeks.

The barbershop closed over on Maple, he said and I saw his
front teeth were gone, the front of his gums swollen and red.

Well, there's still Danny Morgan doing haircuts over on Hannaford, I told him, confused about what was going on, why that
barbershop on Maple was the first thing we were talking about
after all these months silently sharing this house. I wondered if
I'd misunderstood, having not had my coffee yet, and startled to
find him sitting this way, in front of the door at six a.m.

If you want, I offered, you could give yourself a free haircut
with the scissors in the kitchen, too, use the—

Nah, I don't need no haircut, he interjected, and I glimpsed
how his gums had swollen around the dents where his front teeth
had been.

All right, I said, you were the one who brought up the barbershop.

I hoped it wasn't showing on my face, how intense it felt to see
him again, and in such a miserable state, with his front lip sunken
in such an ugly way, his hair and his hands so filthy.

I meant for that tower of yours that isn't standing upright, he
said, and it pained me to hear the faint, labored whistling he had
to do for the letter *s* with no front teeth for his tongue to push

against. He explained the barbershop had put out the bases of their barber chairs last night on the curb. They're steel and heavy, he said, with a cylinder in the middle you could probably weld somehow—

Yes, I get it, I told him. You mean with the cylinder up inside the bottom box to keep the tower upright. Aren't you something, Hounslow!

I shuffled down the rest of the steps, to get closer to him in my excitement until I saw him flinch. I stopped about a foot away, where the floorboards began to sink slightly toward the middle of the room. Under my slippers, I felt the tilt of the wood, some sort of gunk on the floor.

How many did you see on the curb? I asked and he said just three, or that was all he saw the barbershop had put out last night.

Last night? Oh shit, I said and darted to the doormat where I kept my snow boots, sure somebody else had likely grabbed the bases already, until Elliott assured me there was no need to rush out, that he'd hidden all three under an abandoned truck parked nearby, too smashed for anyone to drive anywhere. I asked if he was sure nobody would spot them under the truck and he nodded.

They should be there, he said, and I felt a welcome warmth pour all through me at the thought of the effort he must have gone to last night, dragging those heavy steel chair bases under a truck in such a harsh wind and the temperature in the single digits.

I think you may be the closest to a benefactor these towers are ever gonna get, I told him, and thanked him for the mirrors he'd left by the door the other day, too.

Still hunched on the floor like a pile of discarded clothes, he shrugged, and said he liked what I was doing with the mirrors. I wouldn't have thought of somethin' like that, he said. And you just fuckin' did it.

Want some coffee? I asked, out of practice with conversation, with compliments, with anything really, other than talking to my towers.

Given the terrible last time we were together in the kitchen, I didn't have the nerve to look at Elliott on the way down the hall or once we reached the kitchen either. I went straight to the faucet and filled the kettle, kept my back to him as I got out the instant Folgers, aware of his unease behind me, and the new potato chips now sitting where the stolen bag had been.

I'm sorry about your teeth, I said, keeping my back to him, pouring a teaspoon of coffee into his mug and my own.

I heard him sigh behind me, the chair squeak as he moved it a little closer or farther away. I didn't turn around until the kettle was steaming and I'd filled our cups. At the table, Elliott had one hand pressed over his mouth and I told him it was none of my business what had happened to his teeth, that there was no need to tell me. I'm just sorry is all, I said. That you lost them.

It's all right, he said, and again I heard the sad faint whistle on his *s*. If somebody was coming into my house every night, he said, I'd want to know who kicked their teeth in, too, but you don't have to worry. A friend of mine was just being an asshole.

Some friend, I said, setting down his coffee in front of him and backing away, toward the other end of the table.

Elliott tucked a hunk of his filthy hair behind his ear, then started gnawing on the raw skin around his right thumb, saying nothing for a moment. Then he began talking again in the halting manner of his that had become familiar, as if he didn't trust anything he said to be right. He explained he hadn't seen it coming at all, this friend who kicked his teeth in. My sister never liked him, he explained. Chris was always asking her what she thought was good at Taco Bell, but everyone at school did that.

Elliott paused, looking down at his coffee, and explained Chris had lived down the road from them, the only other kid his age within walking distance of the house that Manuel, his stepfather, had built for them. I asked if Chris was in that crew of his on Burton Rock and he said yes, that Chris was the tall one who'd been driving the ATV, and who'd driven him around all of high school. Elliott told me this looking down at the chipped edge of the kitchen table, picking with his finger at the crud that had lodged inside the chipped wood. He told me Chris had picked him up every morning, and also took Jackie sometimes, once his stepdad got too sick to drive and his mother was working. He said Chris's family had all come to Manuel's funeral and it hadn't seemed to matter too much, Chris wanting to make the same annoying Taco Bell jokes to Jackie or talking shit about Mexicans.

I didn't think Chris would go to that fuckin' rally in Deerfield, he said.

Did he just want to stand around, I asked, with a bunch of deaf old KKK dragons who haven't died yet?

That's not what it was, Elliott said, and explained the rally was huge, with hundreds of younger people.

Jesus, I said and he nodded, hiding the sunken skin of his upper lip against the rim of his mug.

I curled my toes inside my slippers. I'd been surprised at how many signs had gone up all of a sudden for such a man to be president. Every time I went to the Giant Eagle, there were more bumper stickers with his dumb name. I saw more Confederate flag stickers, too, which I'd rarely seen anywhere except on the creep tables at the flea markets—whoever showed up peddling used porn mags usually sold some Confederate flag crap along with the boob shots. I'd listened to one uppity newscaster on TV throwing around the words *white supremacy* like Leah had in the truck. I had to click away to another channel, imagining Leah off in New York sinking deeper into her judgment of me, her decision to scrub me out of her life like I was a character stain.

Is that why he kicked you in the face, I asked, for not wanting to go to the rally?

Elliott shook his head, said he'd kept riding around with Chris after the rally, that the problem had happened in the parking lot of Pizza Hut, when they'd run into his sister and a friend of hers.

Chris just kept talkin' shit, Elliott said. He got right up in my sister's face and I tried, I tried to pull that fucker back. Jackie and her friend were both crying and it was just . . . Elliott pressed his lips together, shook his head.

I asked if the rest of his crew had come after him, too, and he shrugged, made a sound like he'd gotten the wind blown out of him just sitting at the table, thinking about it. I asked how his sister and her friend were doing now and he said Jackie hated leaving her aunt's house, even for school, and his mom was a wreck.

They don't want me getting involved, that's for fuckin' sure, he said, pushing his mug away, and I told him I was sorry, that his family would surely forgive him after a few months and let it go.

Elliott shook his head and said he wasn't sure, that he'd just stood there, hoping Chris would stop. He'd done nothing until Chris spit in his sister's face. And spit in her friend's face.

Oh Elliott, I said, and once again the crumbling feeling of rot giving way in the kitchen came over me, same as that day Elliott came in half dressed, grabbed me through my shirt, and it was so dreadful that I hoped the floor might fall away and remove any need to say a single word more to each other, for termites to just surge up and eat the house around us, devour the old floor under our feet, eat up all the moldy cabinet shelves and chew them into oblivion. There's really no telling, is there, I said, what kind of horrible a person can turn out to be.

You were the one who asked, Elliott said, tipping back in my wooden kitchen chair, and I hoped the two hind legs wouldn't collapse on him. Tilted back in it, he assured me I didn't have to worry about him bringing any drugs or assholes into my house at night, that he would just be coming here on his own.

You can come in anytime, I offered and he nodded with a tense expression, said we'd better go for the chair bases before somebody spotted them under the truck. I agreed and got up, but the suck of his despair was too strong for me to pull myself away from the table. Pressed against the table's edge, I told him about

Leah wanting to get the hell away from that crew of his, too, her calling them racists and white supremacists. It was a shock to hear so much talk all of a sudden about what had always gone over as normal here, the expectation to just put up with people's bigotry like you do a flare of a pain in your skull, hoping it'll go away, isn't the tumor that will keep on getting bigger till you can't remember your own name.

I felt an ache in my own skull picturing it, that idiot from the cliff spitting in Jackie's pretty face. It was too sickening to dwell on for long, and yet there was the sunken, ugly new shape to Elliott's upper lip right in front of me, his knocked-out teeth a testament to the direction things were going with that man running for president, blaming Mexicans for the unemployment here, his name multiplying on the roadside like clumps of poison ivy.

I'll be back, all right? I told Elliott and he nodded, getting up as well now from the table. Upstairs, I splashed some water on my face and brushed my teeth, and an idea came to me on the toilet as sometimes ideas do. I made my stiff way back downstairs and found Elliott sitting on the floor again, next to the front door.

You know what's going to be beautiful? I asked him and he didn't hazard a guess. What's going to be beautiful, I said, is not shooting Chris and making his foul heart bleed. It's going to be hauling one of these towers outside and blasting an unexpected hole right through it. I've been wanting to do something with bullets. What do you think?

Shit, Jean, you just get crazier all the time, Elliott laughed, cracking open the front door as his answer, letting in a sudden rush of light, both of us still fumbling with our coats, still holding the despair we'd come to in the kitchen, but at least we had a reason to keep on moving, the possibility of welding something a little better than who we were a second ago. Sculpture, Louise said, being a chance to fix what you can't in your prima materia, whatever monstrousness lurks so deep in your marrow there is no getting it out entirely.

Outside, the cold bit right through my wool jacket. I saw Elliott wince, too, in his puffy black coat torn at the elbow, and the front zipper looked broken. An open coat like that didn't promise much of a chance against the cold we were having this week. Both truck doors had iced shut overnight and required quite a bit of swearing and tugging to jerk them open. Once we finally managed to climb into the cabin, we got hit with the deeper cold trapped inside, severe as the exhale of a freezer bin.

You've got more to offer than you think, Hounslow, I declared, my teeth chattering unstoppably. We're gonna weld the hell out of those chair bases, I told him, and it doesn't matter if nobody ever sees what we do with them. You've got a gift, okay? You saw those chair bases on the curb and got an idea so strong you did something about it. That urge will keep you alive. You have to choose not to be dead, you hear what I'm saying? Not! To! Be! Dead! I shouted, whacking the steering wheel with my hand, my palm so cold I could barely feel the bang of it against the wheel.

Well, we will be dead, Elliott said, if you don't start the fuckin' truck and get the heat going.

Oh, I won't let you freeze to death, I told him. I might set the house on fire, though, that's always a possibility.

Fire would be fine, Elliott said, blowing his breath into his cupped hands while I started the engine. Backing up, pockets of ice in the driveway cracks clinked under the tires like the ground itself was cracking awake and we were shattering something, daring to set out in this truck for something as useless as a new tower of Manglements. It felt wonderfully outrageous, setting out this early on a day this freezing, heading past the same derelict rows of houses, which held almost no one now. Hardly anyone sleeping or dreaming—just a frozen void of morning world to drive into, make our way together to the corner of Henley, where the barbershop sat dark now as well.

Elliott showed me the abandoned truck at the curb that he'd used as a hiding spot. The truck looked corroded enough to have been hauled up like a body from the bottom of a creek. The windshield was smashed, the front seats both ripped out, and the back ones busted open like buzzards had mistaken them for stomachs and tore up the foam guts with their beaks. There was nothing in that vehicle's abject state to draw anyone's attention to the possibility of somebody having stashed anything under it. Elliott was right.

Shivering beside him, I bent to take a look and gasped. The metal chair base was just the thing to get that leaning tower to stay erect, and the other two would be magnificent to add some extra stability to the next towers, to add something new—that moved, maybe. This street certainly needed something that moved. We could add a few wheels, maybe, like that artist with the big mobiles whose name I couldn't remember—and couldn't look up either, with no laptop, though I didn't say that aloud to Elliott. What would it help, when he'd just gone to great lengths in the freezing cold to stash these barber chair bases for me? I told him about adding a wheel to the top of the next tower, about playing around with something that whirled and came alive, and he nodded.

I could find a few bike wheels easy enough, he offered, the air so cold the words clouded in front of his mouth and in front of mine as well, when I said what an idea, Hounslow, wouldn't a bike wheel be just the right size and weight. I kept on talking, enjoying the fleeting sight of our words in the frigid air, shivering there next to that sad corpse of a truck and the newly dead barbershop.

And yet there were our words still forming clouds, proof that something more might happen on this street. There was no reason it couldn't be the two of us welding more towers, trying to make Art with a capital *A* because there was nobody to say otherwise, to stop us from hauling these chair bases into my truck bed, speeding from the emptied stores on Henley to the emptied houses on Paton Street, no reason to speed at this hour except to feel our own forward motion, heading home to the glorious pleasure of erecting something new.

LEAH

I read an intriguing theory last night, on mourning the loss of a complicated person. It is a method that does not involve repeating a name or seeking relief in the conjuring of fairy tales. In Spanish, the Chilean writer Alejandro Jodorowsky calls the method psicomagia. If someone dies and leaves you in a state of petrifying incoherence, Jodorowsky recommends igniting some symbolic object—a chair where that complicated person used to preside, or maybe a hat that baffling person used to wear.

The chosen act of psychic release, however, does not necessarily have to involve flames and destruction. Psychomagic, according to Jodorowsky, can also happen with an act of preservation. The reupholstering by hand, for example, of a chair belonging to the person whose voice won't let go of you, imposing a new color over the chair's unchangeable shape, a brighter fabric of your own choosing.

A friend in Peru sent this method of Alejandro Jodorowsky's to me after I told her about my ongoing emails to galleries and museums. I expressed my confusion about why I was going to all this effort, which was most likely futile, as nobody had taken interest yet in the massive sculptures that my stepmother hadn't meant to leave to me. Whether I sent more emails or made more phone calls, I had a feeling the outcome wouldn't change. I wondered if I was only continuing with the calls to distract myself from grieving, and my friend asked whether the calls on behalf of Jean's towers were my way of grieving.

There are no rules, she said, for what form grieving has to take. Why couldn't futile calls and emails be as valid a form of grief as sitting in passive silence, or opening a box of matches and setting a chair on fire?

For the sake of this tale, let's say perhaps the calls and emails might not be futile. Let's say something more might happen and Jean's sculptures will not end up in a scrapyard. Let's say her intricately welded boxes and capsules will not eventually end up crushed in the mechanical hands of a grapple, her towers flattened like discarded car doors.

For Jean's sake, and for my own coherence, I will not move on with my life just yet, will not give up and let her spike-covered sculptures, her rusty halos made of bike wheels, sink through the floor in that house with Elliott. I know there's no shortage of stories in these mountains full of rage, hatred, and murder, but let's say this tale about Jean living with Elliott, assembling these towers, might end another way. Let's say whatever happened between them involved some rage, desperation, and at least one robbery, but maybe something else occurred as well, working together on this forsaken street, talking about Agnes Martin and making elaborate metal sculptures for no one at all.

Let's say not all my emails go ignored. At a gallery in Cincinnati, an intern with time to spare decides to click on the photos of the towers and likes them enough to pass the images along to another intern she knows at the Southern Alleghenies Museum of Art. Let's say the photos find their way to the curators at this regional museum, who are intrigued enough to drive to Sevlick and see Jean's sculptures for themselves. They call me to say her sculptures are extraordinary. In my excitement, I stand up out of my chair. When they explain that the removal of them will be prohibitively expensive, I sink back into my seat and ask them why.

To rescue Jean's sculptures from oblivion, the SAMA curators kindly explain, would require the rental of a truck with a telescopic boom lift, and that removal would be possible only after dismantling the roof piece by piece, and then the two ceilings above the living room, and probably pulling off the front of the house as well.

To remove a ceiling and roof with care, instead of just demolishing them, requires expertise. Tearing off a roof, they explain, can be done rather quickly, but to remove it without damaging anything inside requires a longer process, and is not something just any demolition team can do. That cost would be in addition to renting a boom truck, all of which would put things in a price range they can't possibly take on. The well-intentioned curators at the Southern Alleghenies Museum of Art say they are truly sorry. Given their call is about leaving the roof where it is, I don't mention the extra complication of Elliott living in the house.

Two weeks later, however, let's say one of them calls again. He tells me that he can't get Jean's towers out of his mind. He offers to send a photographer and at least exhibit photos of the towers, which leads to a pair of images of Jean's towers in a regional magazine, the sculpture covered with slivers of mirror and the one shot through the chest. They make a striking couple on the page, shot and shimmering together.

A trickle of emails follows, but nobody can afford to dismantle Jean's roof and living room ceiling with the care necessary to avoid damaging the towers. Beyond the roof, there is also the prohibitive cost of the special truck with a boom and horizontal lift strong enough to remove sculptures as massive yet delicate, as prone to breakage, as Jean's spike-covered towers with all their capsules, their fragile bicycle-wheel halos. To transport the towers in proper slat crates to keep them intact on the turnpike would require at least two box trucks, possibly more.

Let's say a global pandemic happens soon after. A year and a half of rust begins to bloom around the welds on the towers. Elliott stays on in the house, finds a naval jelly used to remove rust from the hulls of boats, and does what he can to keep the rust from blooming outward, from one box to another. Jean's capsules, too, start to tarnish and the floorboards crack under one of the heavier towers.

Let's say the country cracks as well, the floor gives way to a new era, or at least the prospect of one. We watch hordes of armed people storming one of the most important government buildings in the country. Their faces appear on the news while I'm making a frittata. One of the first heavily armed people arrested is from Sevlick. The name of the town where I was born appears in red capital letters under the man's name. To see SEVLICK in all caps under the arrest news brings back the red capital letters on Jean's one horizontal sculpture, extending long as a body on the floor, her red letters that spelled out TRIAN-GULATION OF THE SELF.

That January when the storming of the government building occurs, Jean's living room floor begins to rot and warp under her sculptures. A coldness enters, and also mice. Elliott sends a brief text in February that he's moved out. He doesn't tell me where he went, only that I will have to take care of the house now, until I figure out what to do about Jean's towers.

For weeks at a time, I do nothing about them. I stop thinking about them for days until I'm walking somewhere alone, which doesn't happen often. During most of my waking hours, I find it possible to push away the thought of Jean's towers still hidden in her distant house, the floor rotting out beneath them. I focus on Silvestre and Gerardo, on my editing jobs and going to protests, until I run out alone for a carton of eggs, or oat milk, and the towers come back to me—the wonder and undeniable beauty of them, their survival feeling inextricable from my own vitality.

In the tentative new era the country has entered, we return to Jean's house in the spring to find the towers covered in spiderwebs that stick to our hands when we step inside. To avoid getting spiderwebs in our mouths, we have to make swimming motions with our arms to move through the webbed-over areas of the room. I turn and find my son licking the sticky webs of my step-mother's house from his lips and urge him not to ingest anything here. I warn him about the questionable particles in this room from Jean's welding and from the mold rotting the floors.

With Elliott gone, we decide to check things upstairs and

find a newly broken window in the master bedroom, more bats hissing upside down in that bedroom where Jean's parents slept than I can bear to describe.

Once we rush back downstairs, away from the bats, swim our arms back through the living room into the silence outside, we find a local company to board over her windows and reinforce the floor with new planks. Gerardo asks them to add support jacks under the old floorboards to help sustain the weight of the sculptures that haven't sunk yet. I text Elliott to let him know we checked on the house and the towers. I receive a reply from somebody named Mandy who's taken over the number.

When I tell Gerardo, he sits with the news for a moment, before responding that we don't always get to find out what happens to people, or who they really are. I agree this is true, though I can't let go of the question of Elliott, what actually transpired in that house between him and Jean.

The present, however, keeps on insisting on my attention regardless. Soon after that second family trip to Sevlick, we have a second child. On maternity leave, while the new baby sleeps, I renew my efforts to find someone who knows someone who might know someone who might take an interest in what Jean slipped to her death to create.

More months and rust accrue. None of the emails make anything happen, until the same tenacious director from the Southern Alleghenies Museum of Art writes, the one who oversaw the photograph exhibit of Jean's sculptures two years ago. He asks where the sculptures have gone and I tell him they've gone nowhere, that they are filling with mice. He replies that he is sorry to hear this, and I tell him I'm sorry, too. Our brief email exchange feels like an ending.

Let's say it's not the end, however. There is a museum in Baltimore I've never heard of that is devoted to astonishing art happening beyond the usual established paths. It's called the American Visionary Art Museum and its founder comes across the photos of Jean's towers. She decides to take a trip to the house and tells me the towers aren't ruined and she will find a way to save them. She finds donors and rallies board members.

Once again, two months later, I return with my family in another rental car to Sevlick to watch a crew rip the rotting roof off Jean's home in expert pieces. They are methodical in their demolishing, peeling back each layer of the house until they reach the ceiling above the towers. The process takes days and my children get restless.

Finally, the boom truck arrives on Jean's forsaken street. A giant, cranelike apparatus on a flatbed truck comes beeping toward us, past one crumbling home after another, past all the pillars fallen like rotten tree trunks across the other porches. A few people follow the immense shiny boom truck in their cars. It is a small, odd parade of drivers who roll down their windows and ask what's happening. I tell them my stepmother lived here, that she welded sculptures in this house and they are headed to the museum for American visionaries.

To the what? Whatever, craziest goddamn country, one man says and takes off.

Another driver just nods, asks for Jean's name, squints at me for a few seconds in silence before pulling away.

The transfer of the towers into the trucks goes into the evening and I open Jean's garage for the children to play with their toys. Some weed I don't recognize, with tiny purple flowers, has grown up through the cracked floor where Jean waged her epic battles with her father. Alongside her now decapitated home, while the extraction of her spectacular towers continues, the garage feels eerily unaltered, a chamber outside time. Jean's father's tin soup cans still line the floor, full of the same nails. The same rusted fire pail holds his now ancient tins of Altoids. Standing in front of that corroded fire pail, the beeps of the boom truck in the driveway obscuring my voice, I summon my stepmother. *Goodbye, Jean*, I tell her. *Please don't haunt me for the rest of my life.*

Of course, I know this plea is futile. She will haunt me anyhow, and whatever I read aloud to my children, whatever I concoct in my mind, some bit of Jean will rise in my voice. I'll never be free of this cluttered garage, the nails my stepmother chucked at her father and which he chucked right back, refusing to weld a stool with any flair of imagination, to attempt any artistic risk that might raise questions about who people expected him to be.

For this fairy tale, let's say no rusted spikes fall off Jean's towers before they reach the museum in Baltimore. Let's say the museum will provide, for a brief time, a full circumference of open gallery space around each one, allowing viewers to take in her capsules and stacks of boxes from every possible angle. Never more than a few people at a time will stop to consider them. No line will form around the corner. After a few months of the exhibit, most of her towers will go into the museum's storage building, except for two, which will be placed in a new redbrick building for larger works. They will be installed next to a dazzling car someone covered with shards of blue glass bottles, seashells, and cream-colored buttons.

Let's say the two towers of Jean's kept on permanent display will be the same pair that appeared in the regional magazine, the one with the bullet hole and the other covered with a mosaic of mirrors. Shot and shimmering, those two towers will remain next to a plaque with the date of Jean's birth in Sevlick and her death in the same place. The plaque will also provide a few sentences about her job in the billing department at the county hospital until it closed, the nine years of her marriage, the child from that time who became her daughter.

Before the lone full exhibit of all the towers closes, let's say something else might occur. A solitary person will shuffle into the main building and behold Jean's towers for a long time, a person who has a craving to make a large sculpture but has lacked the gall to try. A person who has told hardly anyone about this desire and who will study Jean's Manglements with great focus, intrigued by the metal platforms that help keep the stacks of boxes from falling, and the odd heavy bases made from barber chairs.

Let's say this person will feel a little bolder after peering into Jean's curious capsules, spotting the sawed-off plastic soldier torsos inside them with their acorn heads. Let's say this person will find the audacious sense of play Jean brought to her towers late in life so alluring and freeing that they will start pulling over to consider discarded objects on the curb. Let's say this person will carry some of the discards to the car and then into the house, where they will begin assembling a sculpture of their own.

ACKNOWLEDGMENTS

I couldn't have written this novel without studying welding with the outstanding metal artists Julia Murray and Norman Ed, and with Dan Neville at the Center for Metal Arts, in Pennsylvania. Helen Golubic, the pursuit of unexpected beauty in this novel belongs to you.

I researched the work of Agnes Martin and Louise Bourgeois in numerous sources, but the quotes from Agnes Martin referred to in the novel mostly come from a 1992 German/English bilingual edition of Martin's writing published with Cantz and edited by Herausgegeben von Dieter Schwarz. The majority of the quotes from Louise Bourgeois come from her volume of writings *Destruction of the Father / Reconstruction of the Father: Writings and Interviews 1923–1997*, published by MIT Press and edited by Marie-Laure Bernadac and Hans-Ulrich Obrist.

To my extraordinary agent and editor, PJ Mark and Laura Tisdel, thank you for your expert guidance and for your caring presence through every phase of every novel. Thank you to Andrea Schulz, Jenn Houghton, and everyone at Viking and Janklow & Nesbit. To Rumaan Alam, Angie Cruz, Patricia Engel, Garth Greenwell, Cathy Park Hong, Adriana Jacobs, Gerry Jonas, Katy Lederer, Raven Leilani, Alex Mar, Marie Matsuki Mockett, Steve O'Connor, Devan Sipher, and Rene Steinke, thank you for your superb insights and suggestions, for the vitality of your voices on the page and on the phone.

Primal thanks to my mother and to my stepmother, to my father and to my sisters, Rebecca and Robin Grace, to my nieces, Ignacia and Antonia, for joining our family during the pandemic, to Jesthel, Jeff, and Jim for holding us close, and to all the friends and relatives on various continents who supported this novel and the books before it.

A Leo y mis hijos, que suerte amanecer con ustedes.